Rekindled
Dallas Fire & Rescue

by Paige Tyler

D1010376

Cover Design by Kim Killion Designs

Things are about to get hot in here...

When firefighter Jax Malloy gets called out to battle a blaze at a hotel in the middle of the night, he doesn't expect to find the sister of his best friend and fellow firefighter in need of rescuing. He didn't even know she was back in Dallas.

Skye Chandler has always had a crush on Jax and is ready to be more than friends. All they have to do is survive an overprotective brother who just doesn't get it, and a psychotic ex-boyfriend who'd rather see her dead than with another man.

Chapter One

JAX MALLOY BRACED himself with a hand on the door as Tory Wilcox whipped Station 58's big fire engine around the last ninety degree turn. They then headed down Jacobs Street toward the burning hotel just ahead of them. It was midnight and he was still a little groggy from the catnap he'd been taking, but one look at the inferno raging through the building woke him right up. The place was a nightmare come to life.

"Stations 34 and 15 are still five minutes out with their engines and ladder trucks. We'll set our lines on the west side of the building to try to keep this from spreading until they get here," Lieutenant Nate Boone said, glancing over his shoulder at Jax from the front passenger seat. "Malloy, you and Wilcox are on rescue until backup arrives."

"Roger that," Jax said, already buckling up his turn-out gear and running through a mental checklist of all the equipment he and Tory would need before heading in.

The moment the engine lurched to a stop near the west corner of the hotel, he was out of the vehicle and running for the compartments on the side of the engine. He had his self-contained breathing apparatus on by the time Tory ran around the back side of the truck. Almost as tall as Jax, he had dark blond hair and a lean, wiry build. Jax helped Tory get his pack on, then they quickly took turns checking each other's turn-out gear and equipment to make sure both were good to go.

Jax just turned to head for the hotel when a uniformed officer ran up, breathing hard and sweating like crazy. His clothes were smudged with gray and black ash.

"There are at least three more people on the upper floors, maybe more," the cop gasped. "I tried to get to them, but the smoke was too thick. The whole western stairwell is burning above the third floor."

Jax nodded. "Thanks. We got it from here." He jerked his chin at the hotel guests who had already gotten out. "Move those people across the street farther down the block. If the roof collapses, it's gonna be bad."

The officer nodded and took off. Jax grabbed his fire axe and slipped it into the holder on his belt, then jogged toward the building, Tory beside him. The engines and ladder trucks from 15 and 34 rolled up just as they pulled on their masks. Jax turned on his bottle and entered the building.

"Lieutenant, this is Malloy," Jax shouted into his radio. "Tory and I are going up the east side stairwell. We have a report of people trapped on the upper floors."

"Roger that. Watch yourselves up there."

Running up steps while wearing a self-contained breathing apparatus, helmet, and fire-resistant turn-out suit that weighed an extra sixty pounds wasn't exactly fun, but as a firefighter, Jax was used to it. He automatically controlled his breathing so he could conserve as much air in his self-contained breathing apparatus as possible, and kept humping up the smoke-filled stairwell. The SCBA gave him a full thirty minutes in ideal conditions, but conditions in a burning building were about as far from ideal as you could get. The fire was already eating through the walls above him, and the ceiling didn't look like it was far behind. The hotel had ten minutes tops before it was completely devoured by flames.

He and Tory almost tripped over an older man down on his knees on the third-floor landing. His equally older wife was at his side, urging him to get to his feet. The woman's shoulders sagged with relief at the sight of them.

Jax was all set to help her while Tory assisted her husband, but she waved away his hand.

Paige Tyler

"There's a young woman up on the fifth floor. She helped us down, then went back up looking for other people," she said, her voice hoarse from the smoke. "I can walk down. You go find her."

Jax glanced at Tory to see him pressing the mask of his air pack against the old man's face. Splitting up once you went inside a burning building wasn't smart, but sometimes it had to be done.

"You good?" he asked.

His fellow firefighter nodded. "Go. I'll get these two down by relay if I have to."

Giving Tory a nod, Jax sprinted up the stairs. A moment later, he heard Tory's voice on the radio, announcing he was coming down with two, while Jax was heading up for another.

By the time Jax reached the fifth floor, he knew the chances of finding anyone alive up there were slim. All public places like this were supposed to have sprinklers and water deluge systems, but if the hotel had them, they weren't working. He could feel the heat from the flames even with all his gear on, and knew the air was getting hot enough to sear lung tissue. He kept going, though. He'd seen miracles too many times to give up on anyone.

Ten steps later, he almost stumbled over a woman lying on the floor. She had a wet bath towel over her shoulders, and another draped over her head. Smart girl, he thought as he crouched down beside her. He was half afraid he was too late, but then the woman coughed. Wrapping one arm around her, Jax gently pulled her up into a sitting position, then took off his mask to place it over her nose and mouth, pushing the button on the regulator to dump extra air into it.

He would have preferred to wait to see if the woman was able to breathe, but he couldn't risk it. The building could give way any minute. So instead, he got the mask on the girl's head as well as he could with her long hair, then scooped her into his arms and headed for the stairwell.

The smoke burned his throat like acid as he carried her down the five flights of stairs, but he ignored it. Another crew of firefighters were heading up as he came down, and he gave them a nod as he maneuvered around them, then through what was left of the lobby and out the front door. Damn, fresh air never tasted so good.

"Malloy. Out of the building with one rescue," he called over his radio as he hurried over to the collection of Dallas Rescue vehicles and regular ambulances set up on the far side of Jacobs street. There were at least a dozen other patients already there, sitting on gurneys or on the ground. Most had oxygen masks on, getting good air into their lungs. Jax saw the older couple he'd left with Tory in the stairwell, but there was no sign of the other firefighter. He'd probably already gone back inside.

Alec McIntyre, one of the paramedics from Jax's station immediately ran over, a green oxygen tank with a mask kit already attached in his hand. Jax gently placed the woman on the ground, then turned off the valve on the top of his tank and took the big firefighter's face mask away. Alec quickly replaced it with the smaller medical mask. The woman was aware enough to get her hands around it and press it firmly to her face, breathing deep.

"I've got her," Alec said, already checking the woman for burns and other injuries.

Jax was about to turn around and head back to the burning hotel when the woman flipped her long, brunette hair aside to fit the oxygen mask more closely to her face. Jax stared, stunned.

"Skye, is that you?" he asked.

He was sure he was wrong even as he said the words. No way could the slim, curvy girl sitting on the curb be the little sister of his best friend and fellow firefighter, Dane Chandler. Three years younger than them, Skye had spent most of their childhood running around behind them wanting to be included in everything they did. He hadn't seen her in years, not since he'd graduated high school and moved away. Skye had only been a freshman in high school then, all skinny arms, long legs, knobby knees, and sharp elbows.

The woman blinked up at him, her big, blue eyes going wide as they filled with recognition. Damn, it was her. Little Skye had grown up, and even through all the dirt and grime he couldn't miss the fact that she'd become one hell of a beautiful woman.

She pulled the oxygen mask away, giving him a glimpse at full lips and the cute, upturned nose he remembered. "Jax?"

Skye probably would have said more, but the paramedic knelt down and put the mask on her face again. Over the radio in Jax's ear, the lieutenant was ordering everyone to the west side of the structure—they were about to lose containment.

All Jax could do was give her a nod before turning to race for the west side of the hotel. The flames along the roof were threatening to jump over to the next building, and two ladder trucks were using their elevated hoses to douse the upper floor. Jax quickly moved over to help two other firefighters working a two-and-a-half inch attack hose as they tried to get water on the second and third floors.

Working a hose together like this took a lot of focus at the best of times. The volume of water coming through it could throw a team to the ground if they weren't careful. But as he synched his movements with the other two men, he couldn't help but wonder what the hell Skye was doing staying in a hotel and not with her brother. Hell, Dane hadn't even mentioned his sister was back in Dallas.

Jax told himself to put thoughts of Skye and her sudden appearance in town on the back burner. They had a fire to fight.

Chapter Two

IT TOOK MORE than an hour before they were able to get the worst of the blaze under control, and by the time Jax had a chance to check on Skye, she'd already been taken to the local hospital along with everyone else who had sucked in too much smoke.

"Shit," he muttered.

He'd wanted to see how she was doing before they took her to get checked out. Dane had traded shifts with another firefighter so he could ride in a rodeo fundraiser for the Dallas Fire Fighters Association, and he knew his friend would freak out when he discovered his little sister had been in a fire.

"Something wrong?"

Jax turned to see Lieutenant Boone behind him, a concerned expression on his weathered face.

"The woman I pulled off the fifth floor is Dane's sister," he said.

9

The lieutenant's hazel eyes widened. "Damn. How bad is she hurt?"

Jax shook his head. "She seemed okay, but I don't know for sure. She was almost unconscious by the time I got to her and she definitely sucked in a lot of smoke."

Nate frowned. "Dump your gear on the truck, then get over to the hospital and find out how bad it is. Don't say a word to anyone else until you talk to Dane. Let me know what's going on as soon as you can."

Jax nodded and jogged over to the fire engine to drop off his turn-out gear. He'd just finished stowing everything in one of the equipment lockers on the side of the truck when he spotted Kole Brandt, one of the other firefighters from his station.

"Hey, Brandt. I need to run to the hospital to check on the woman I got out of the building. Can you take care of my gear?"

Kole didn't gripe about the extra gear to clean, or the fact that the rest of the engine crew would be one man short dealing with the aftermath of the blaze, but simply nodded. Every firefighter knew what it was like to worry about someone who'd been hauled out of a burning building.

"Hope whoever you're checking on is okay," Kole called as Jax jogged over to where the uniformed officers were still working crowd control.

Jax had planned on asking the first cop he ran into for a ride to the station when he recognized the officer who'd pointed him and

Tory toward the east stairwell earlier. The nametag on his chest read Perry.

"Think you can give me a lift back to the firehouse?" he asked the cop. "I need to get to the hospital to check on someone I pulled from the building."

"Sure, no problem."

Thanks to the flashing lights, Perry got him back to Station 58 in less than ten minutes. Jax wished he could grab a quick shower to get the smell of smoke off, but he didn't want to take the time. So instead, he jumped in his pickup, then sped out of the parking lot and headed for the hospital.

He called Dane on the way, but it went to voicemail. No shock there. It was the frigging middle of the AM. Any rational human would be sleeping like a log. Not wanting to freak Dane out any more than he had to, he kept the message short and optimistic.

"Hey, Dane. It's Jax," he said. "We just rolled on a hotel fire on Jacobs. Your sister was there and sucked down some smoke, but she's going to be okay. I'm heading over to see her now at Parkland Emergency. Call me as soon as you get this."

Luckily, the roads were deserted, so it didn't take long for Jax to get to the hospital. He found a parking space, then hauled ass for the entrance. As he ran inside, he prayed he was right about Skye being okay. Smoke inhalation was dangerous as hell, and while Skye had seemed fine when he'd carried her

11

out of the fire, that didn't mean she was fine now.

Jax was all prepared to sweet-talk his way past the nurse on duty to get in to see Skye, but fortunately, Emily Cartwright, the gray-haired woman behind the desk, knew him. She was used to seeing him bringing in patients, and seemed surprised he was alone.

"A woman the paramedics brought in a little while ago from that hotel fire on Jacobs is the sister of one of the firefighters I work with. I just wanted to check on her," he explained. "Her name is Skye Chandler."

Emily nodded. "I remember them bringing her in. Hang on a minute and I'll take a look at her chart."

Picking up the reading glasses dangling from a chain around her neck, she perched them on the bridge of her thin nose and moved closer to her computer. Jax had to force himself not to lean over the counter so he could see the monitor. Instead, he waited impatiently while she tapped at the keys.

"Oh yes, here she is," Emily said. "She inhaled a lot of smoke and she's been on oxygen since she came in, but she's going to be fine. In fact, the doctor will be releasing her in a little while."

Jax breathed a sigh of relief. Thank God.

"Can I see her?" he asked.

Emily gave him a smile that was all too knowing. "Down the hall. She's in the fourth bay on the right."

He thanked her, then made his way past the first three bays. He stopped outside the fourth and peeked around the curtain. Skye was half lying, half sitting back on the exam table, her eyes closed and an oxygen tube under her nose. She was still wearing the soot-smudged jeans and T-shirt she had on when he found her. Her breathing was so slow and steady that for a moment Jax thought she was asleep. He was wondering if he should wait outside when she opened her eyes.

"Jax!"

Skye jumped up and ran toward him, completely forgetting the oxygen line attached to her. She almost choked herself with the tubing as she got stopped short a few feet from him, and he quickly stepped forward to help her get untangled.

She laughed and gave him an embarrassed look, her face coloring. He laughed, too. Her voice was a little scratchy from inhaling all that smoke, but other than that, she really did seem fine.

The moment she was free from the oxygen lines, Skye threw her arms around him and hugged him tightly. He hugged her right back. What else was a guy supposed to do when a girl he'd known since she was five years old threw herself into your arms?

But being this close to her reminded him again that his best friend's little sister wasn't so little anymore. Even though he was six-four, Skye came up to his chin now. She had a lot more curves than he remembered her having, too. And some of those very nice curves were pressed up against his chest, letting him know that Skye hadn't taken the time to put on a bra before bolting out of her room during the fire. He had to admit her soft breasts felt damn nice through her thin T-shirt.

And if those thoughts weren't distracting enough, Skye smelled amazing under all the smoke still clinging to her. Like peaches and cream. How the hell was that even possible?

Realizing his cock was starting to harden, he reluctantly took a step back. As happy as he was to see Skye, he had no desire to pitch a boner in front of his best friend's little sister—even if she wasn't so little anymore.

＊ ＊ ＊ ＊ ＊

Skye gave him a small smile as she pushed her hair behind her ear. "Sorry. I didn't mean to tackle you like that. I just can't believe you got me out of that hotel. I thought…"

She couldn't say it out loud. Knowing how close she'd come to dying in that fire made her feel lightheaded and she almost grabbed onto Jax for support. Not that she'd mind putting her hands all over him again. But she didn't want him—or the doctor—thinking she needed to spend the night at the hospital.

14

Jax returned her smile with one that almost made her knees go weak again, for a completely different reason this time.

"Only doing my job," he said. "Good thing I ran into that older couple you helped downstairs. They said you'd gone back up to look for other people."

"I don't even remember falling to the floor up there." Skye resolutely pushed the image out of her mind, preferring to focus on how amazing it had felt to look up when she'd been sitting on the curb and seen Jax standing there. "But then you came swooping in like a superhero and saved me."

Another smile tugged at the corner of his mouth. "I'm not sure about the superhero part. More like just a regular ol' firefighter."

She arched a brow. "Strong, heroic, and humble—sounds like superhero material to me."

Jax chuckled, and Skye decided he had the sexiest laugh she'd ever heard. That made sense since the rest of Jax Malloy was equally sexy.

Skye had never told anyone—well, maybe some of her girlfriends at the time— but she'd had a huge crush on Jax since she was a teenager. Of course, the almost four years in age that separated them meant Jax had never seen her as anything other than his best friend's kid sister. But she'd thought he was the most perfect guy ever.

And he hadn't changed one bit. Same whiskey colored eyes; same thick, dark hair;

same square jaw with just a trace of stubble that she longed to run her fingers over. Same lean muscles.

She wondered if he still rode broncos and bulls at the local rodeo like he'd done back in high school.

Skye stifled a moan at the memory. Just her luck that when she'd finally gotten old enough for things to get interesting, Jax graduated from high school and left Dallas to work on an oil rig in some other part of the state. He never got a chance to see her mature into a woman she'd like to think would have attracted his attention long enough for him to see her as something more than a friend.

Not that it would have mattered because it wasn't long after that when her life had taken a hundred-and-eighty-degree-turn in the other direction. A few years later, she was living in New York City working twelve hour days, and Jax was off doing whatever it was that he'd done. She hadn't even known he was a firefighter until he rescued her tonight. Especially since he and her brother probably worked together.

Then again, she and Dane hadn't talked very much since she'd left.

Yet, here she and Jax were nearly ten years later. She was still thinking how her life might have been different if they'd been more than friends back then when she realized he was talking to her.

She reached for the oxygen tube to hide her embarrassment. "What?"

His hands were gentle as he helped her get it repositioned. "I asked why the heck you went back up to the fifth floor looking for people."

Skye hesitated, pretending to focus on fitting the ends of the tube under nose. The truth was she'd been terrified half to death the moment she woke up and realized the hotel was on fire. She hated fire. So much so that she couldn't even stand to have candles on her birthday cake. When she'd heard the alarm and smelled the smoke, she barely remembered to get dressed and grab her purse before she ran down the stairs and outside.

When she'd gotten to safety, she was afraid to even look back at the building and the flames engulfing it. That was when she heard the cries for help from the hotel, and something inside her had torn open.

Her parents had died in a fire when she was in high school because they couldn't get out of the house after it had filled with smoke. The thought that other people were about to die the same way made her realize she couldn't just leave them in there to burn to death. So she'd somehow swallowed her fear and charged back into the hotel over and over again. She still wasn't sure how she'd done it, or why she'd gone up to the fifth floor when she knew there was no way anyone left up there could still be alive.

"I know I shouldn't have gone back up there that last time," she admitted to Jax with a shrug. "But I couldn't give up until I checked one more time. I didn't want to leave anyone behind."

"That was very brave, and I have no doubt you saved a lot of people's lives." He regarded her in silence, his dark eyes thoughtful. "What were you doing in the hotel in the first place? Why not stay at Dane's place? I know for a fact that he has an extra bedroom. I've crashed there myself a time or two."

Skye stiffened. Running into that burning hotel had been terrifying, but this question scared the hell out of her.

She slowly sank down on the bed. "It's... Well, it's complicated. But I couldn't stay with my brother. Actually, he doesn't even know I'm in town. And I'd rather keep it that way for now."

Jax winced. "That might be a bit tough. I just called and left a message telling him what happened. He's going to know you're here as soon as he listens to it. Sorry."

She gave him a small smile. "It's not your fault. He was bound to find out that I'm back in Dallas sooner or later. I was just hoping to be a bit more settled before I got into everything with him."

Jax frowned. "Skye, are you in some kind of trouble?"

She shook her head. "No, nothing like that, but it's kind of a long story. One I'd rather not get into while sitting in a hospital emergency room."

His mouth tightened, but he didn't press the issue. "Okay. You're obviously working through something, and after the night you just had, you don't need me prying into your business. The nurse said the doctor was ready to release you, so I'll check on that. Where are you going then?"

Skye chewed on her lower lip. "I don't know. Another hotel, I guess. Do you mind giving me a ride?"

"You don't have to stay at another hotel."

"I'm not staying with Dane, if that's what you're going to suggest," she said.

"I wasn't," Jax said. "I was going to say you could stay with me."

Skye hoped her mouth wasn't hanging open. It was just that she had never in a million years expected him to invite her to stay at his place.

"With you?"

"Yeah." He shrugged. "I have an extra bedroom. And unlike Dane, you can stay with me no questions asked."

His invitation was like a godsend. Besides the fact that she was suddenly extremely interested to see what kind of place he lived in, staying with him meant she wouldn't have to spend more money on a hotel. It wasn't like she was destitute, but she didn't want to spend money she didn't have to, just in case her new plans didn't go as smoothly as she hoped.

Okay, no way was she about to look this very attractive gift horse in the mouth. But she also didn't want to cause trouble for Jax, either.

"Are you sure you wouldn't mind? I don't want to get you into hot water with Dane."

"I wouldn't have made the offer if I wasn't sure," Jax said. "You can stay as long as you like. Let me worry about Dane."

For some stupid reason, Skye felt like crying. She'd been living on adrenaline and prayers for about the past two weeks. Things had been tough, to say the least. And that was before the fire in the hotel. But for the first time in a while, it seemed like things were finally looking up. Like maybe fate had decided to throw Jax into her path right when she needed a friend.

Not wanting Jax to see her tears—guys always got so freaked out when a woman cried—she jumped to her feet and hugged him again. But as his big, strong arms came around her and pulled her close to all that muscle, she had to remind herself that he was her brother's best friend. Because right now, the idea of staying at his place had her thinking things she definitely shouldn't be thinking.

Chapter Three

THE NURSE HAD told Skye she'd be free to go after she signed all the paperwork. That had been fifteen minutes ago.

She didn't mean to complain. The medical staff was just doing their job, and on the upside, Jax was sitting beside her while she filled out the forms. But she was getting a bit antsy about Dane showing up and causing a scene. She loved her brother like crazy, but he could be a pain in the ass when it came to trying to tell her what to do all the time. And he was pretty much going to lose his mind when he realized what she'd done. That was why she hadn't called to let him know she was back in Dallas.

Since Jax had left a message on her brother's phone, she knew she was going to have to deal with Dane sooner or later. But after the night she'd had, she would take later rather than sooner.

That was why she practically dragged Jax down the hallway to the hospital's big automatic doors after she'd signed the last form. Unfortunately, they weren't fast enough. Her brother was coming in as they were walking out, and he looked pissed.

"What the hell were you doing in a hotel on Jacobs Street, Skye?"

An inch or two shorter than Jax, her brother had the same stocky build he'd had when he played football in high school, but with even more muscle. Apparently, being a firefighter agreed with him. She only wished he was better at being an older brother. Ever since their parents had died, Dane had taken it upon himself to tell her how to run her life. But those days were over.

"I'm fine, Dane," she said, ignoring his question. "Thank you for asking."

No surprise that her brother hadn't bothered to ask how she was. The way he probably saw it, if she was leaving the hospital, she must be okay. At least he had the good grace to look chagrined.

"I'm sorry." He let out a sigh. "Are you okay?"

She nodded. "Thanks to Jax, yes."

Dane's blue eyes darted to Jax, and something unspoken passed between them before her brother turned back to her.

"What are you doing in Dallas?" he demanded. "And why didn't you call me when you got in?"

Skye didn't want to get into this with Dane now, especially not here in front of Jax and anyone else who might be passing by. But her brother was going to keep badgering her until she answered his questions. And if the only way to get him to stop running her life was to have a knock-down-drag-out right here, then she was damn well going to do it.

"I quit my job in New York to move back here and start my own business," she snapped. "And I didn't call you because you're a jerk."

If Dane was insulted by the jab, he didn't let it show. "What the hell do you mean, you quit? What kind of business could you open up here in Dallas that'll be better than the job you had in New York?"

She folded her arms. "That's not your concern."

She probably sounded like a five-year-old, but she didn't care. Dane didn't get a free pass to run her life because they had the same parents.

The muscle in Dane's jaw flexed. "None of my concern? Dammit, Skye, I didn't waste all my money to send you to college so you could open a business that's sure to fail."

"Thanks for the vote of confidence." Skye clenched her hands into fists, ignoring the way her nails dug into her palms. God, her brother could irritate the crap out of her. "And as for wasting your money, I already paid you back every penny you ever put into my college education. So you don't get to hold that over my head anymore."

Not waiting to see if Jax followed, or even having any idea where he was parked, she pushed past her brother and walked toward the lot. Jax was at her side in two long strides.

"Where the hell are you going?" Dane called.

She should have kept walking, but instead, she turned to face him. He was regarding her with a bewildered expression.

"It's late and I'm tired," she told him. "I'm going to bed."

"My truck is the other way," Dane said.

"I'm not going home with you," she said. "I'm staying with Jax."

If she thought her brother looked pissed before, that was nothing compared to the anger on his face now. "The hell you are."

Muttering something under his breath, Dane started toward them. Skye stood her ground. For all his bluster, Dane would never put a hand on her. He loved her too much for that—even if he did have a funny way of showing it.

Jax, on the other hand, must not have been as sure. He stepped in front of her, blocking Dane's path. Her brother stopped short.

"You need to calm the hell down and take a step back," Jax ordered sharply. "Skye almost died tonight and she doesn't need to deal with your crap right now. Especially not in front of all these people."

Skye felt her face flame. She hadn't even noticed the handful of people in the emergency room who were staring raptly out the window at them like they were watching a freaking episode of Jerry Springer. They might not be able to hear what she and Dane had been saying, but it wasn't hard to figure what was going on between her and her brother. God, this was so embarrassing.

Dane must have been as surprised as she was because he didn't even try to stop them as Jax put his hand on the small of her back, then gently turned her around and pointed her in the direction of a silver four-door pickup. He didn't look back at Dane as he opened the passenger door to let her in, but Skye did. Her brother was standing there with a hard to read expression on his face. Underneath the obvious embarrassment, there was still a lot of anger.

This wasn't over. Not by a long shot.

Turning away, Skye climbed in the truck, then watched Jax walk around the front and get in beside her. Neither of them said anything as he put the truck in gear and pulled out of the parking lot. They'd gone about half a mile when Jax spoke.

"Do you need to stop and get anything from the store?" he asked, his voice soft in the darkness. "Not many places are open at this time of night, but I could probably find something if we drive around."

She glanced at the clock on the dash board. It was after three o'clock in the morning already. She was way too tired to go shopping anyway.

"Any chance you have an extra toothbrush?" Hell, at this point she'd use her finger if that was all she could get. But thankfully, Jax nodded. "That's good enough for tonight. I'll get the other stuff I need tomorrow."

They drove for another thirty minutes, turning down consecutively smaller and smaller roads until they'd left the big buildings and city lights of Dallas far behind. Skye was just about to ask how much farther they had to go when Jax turned into a neatly edged gravel driveway with white paddock fencing on either side. Even though she was tired, she couldn't help sitting up straighter. She'd expected an apartment, or maybe even a townhouse, but it appeared that Jax lived on a real honest-to-goodness ranch.

She turned to look at him. She could just make out his profile in the soft lighting coming from the console. "You live here?"

She shouldn't have been so surprised. Jax had been riding horses and working on ranches since he was kid, so it made sense he'd figured out a way to be around both.

"My grandparents left me the place a few years ago," he said. "It's not much, just a dozen horses and a couple hundred head of cattle. I have a few guys that help me run things when I'm at the station, so most of my money goes to paying them, covering the taxes, and keeping the place maintained. But it's been in the family for generations, so I keep it going."

When Jax stopped his truck in front of the two-story clapboard house with a big wraparound porch, Skye climbed out before he could come around to open the door. In addition to the house, there were two barns and a hay storage building. Even in the dappled moonlight, she could tell that the place was well maintained.

Since the house had belonged to his grandparents, Skye expected the inside to look like something out of *Little House on the Prairie*, but she was surprised to see an open floor plan complete with an updated kitchen that boasted stainless steel appliances, granite countertops, and recessed lighting. The living room was equally modern, complete with a stone fireplace, comfy looking sectional couch, and a big, flat-screen television. If it wasn't for the cowboy, rodeo, and firefighter stuff tastefully sprinkled throughout, she'd think she was in a loft in New York City.

Jax dropped his keys on the table in the entryway just as a black Labrador mix came trotting out from the back of the house to greet him with a wagging tail. Skye smiled as Jax dropped down to a knee and affectionately scratched the dog behind the ears.

"This is Rodeo," he said when he stood up. "Rodeo, meet Skye. She's going to be staying with us."

Rodeo walked over, tail wagging, eager to let her pet him. Skye gladly gave him what he wanted, laughing as he licked her hand.

Jax gave him a pat on the rump. "Okay, Skye's had a long night. Let's give her some space."

Rodeo wagged his tail and obediently trotted into the living room and hopped on the couch. He was absolutely adorable.

"I know you're exhausted, so I'll show you the important stuff and save the nickel tour for later." Jax led her down the main hallway and showed her to a bedroom down the hall from his. "There are three more bedrooms upstairs, but this is the only one I have set up for guests. Bathroom is across the hall. There are toothbrushes, soap, and towels in the linen closet beside the sink. I have some T-shirts in my dresser you can sleep in if you want."

She smiled. "Thanks. Is it okay if I raid your fridge before I go to bed?"

She really wasn't hungry. She was just so wrung out from the argument with Dane that she wasn't sure she could sleep.

"I can make you something to eat while you shower if you want?" he suggested.

She opened her mouth to tell him that wasn't necessary, but then closed it again. Something told her that Jax didn't make offers on a whim. If he was offering, she'd take him up on it.

"Thanks," she said "I won't be long."

He flashed her a smile. "Take your time. I'm going to shower off first anyway. And if one of my T-shirts doesn't work, feel free to look in my closet."

Skye slipped into the bathroom and closed the door. When Jax said there was soap in the linen closet, she'd figured he meant a bar of Ivory, but she was pleased to discover a bottle of body wash. It was the kind marketed specifically for men, but it was still better than a bar of soap. She grabbed a bottle of shampoo, then dumped her smelly clothes on the floor and climbed into the shower.

At first, she simply stood there under the warm spray, more interested in letting it wash away the tension than the dirt. After a few minutes, her shoulders and back relaxed, the water rinsing the stress right down the drain.

Finally feeling up to the task, she went to town with the body wash and shampoo, scrubbing away the smoky stench and black soot that seemed to be everywhere. She ended up washing her hair three times before she felt it was clean enough. As she rinsed out the shampoo, she thought again about how lucky she'd been that night. Not just surviving the fire—though she definitely counted herself blessed there. It was meeting up with Jax. He was probably the only person in the world who could get her strong-willed, determined brother to back off and give her some space. He was also one of the few people she knew who would offer his guest room to a woman he hadn't seen in nearly ten years. There weren't many guys like that in the world.

Deciding she was as clean as she was going to get, she shut off the water and climbed out of the shower. It was as she was drying off that she realized she probably should have grabbed some of Jax's clothes before she showered. Because while Jax had nice soft bath towels, they were barely big enough to wrap all the way around her and have some left over for tucking in.

Well, it was a little late now, so she'd have to make do.

Hoping Jax wouldn't mind if she used his brush, she ran it through her long hair, then readjusted the towel, snuggling it more rightly around her. Holding onto the end she'd tucked in with one hand, she opened the door with the other and poked out her head to make sure Jax was occupied in the kitchen. Then she made a bare-assed naked dash for his bedroom, deciding speed was more important than coverage. Her damp feet made a slapping sound on the hardwood floor, and she prayed she wouldn't slip and bust her butt as she raced for the carpeted room. That was all she needed, to have Jax come running to see what all the noise was about and find her sprawled out naked in his hallway.

But she survived the race to his bedroom, slowing enough to make it inside without falling. She leaned back against the door and looked around the bedroom. There were a lot of dark wood tones to go with the masculine decor, and with the thick drapes meant to block out the light coming through the windows, no one would ever mistake this bedroom for anything than what it was—a man's retreat. But even with all the testosterone-influenced décor, the bedroom still felt cozy. His sleigh bed in particular looked seriously comfortable.

Then again, maybe she was just imagining how comfortable the bed would be if she was in it with Jax.

The thought made her face heat. Jax was a friend, nothing more. No matter how much she was still crushing on him.

She pushed away from the door and wandered over to the chest of drawers against one wall. Jax said she could poke around as much as she wanted so she took him at his word, digging through the dresser until she found those long T-shirts he'd mentioned. She dropped the towel and pulled one on, reveling in how soft it felt against her skin. It smelled good, too—like Jax. But while the T-shirt would definitely work as a sleepshirt, she wasn't so sure it was a good idea to run around in front of Jax out in the kitchen. It easily reached to mid-thigh, but floated up every time she lifted her arms or spun around. And if she bent over for something, Jax would definitely be getting one heck of a show.

Was that why Jax had suggested she wear it, so he could get a show?

Nah. He wasn't like that. Besides, he still saw her as Dane's little sister.

Skye kept the T-shirt on as she wandered into the walk-in closet in case she couldn't find anything better to wear. The closet was perfectly straight and organized, the racks and cubbies full of work and dress uniforms, suits, slacks, jeans, button-downs, dress shirts, and all the shoes and boots a man might want.

She lingered in front of the button-downs for a moment, then moved on to the selection of dress shirts. She was immediately drawn to a crisp white one that seemed extra-long. Inspired, she yanked the T-shirt over her head and tossed it on the bench seat in the middle of the walk-in closet, then slipped into the dress shirt. The moment the fabric settled on her shoulders, she knew she had a winner. She moved over to stand in front of the long mirror as she buttoned it up, turning this way and that just to make sure she wouldn't give Jax an impromptu show-and-tell session. Even though the shirt only hung down a few inches further than the T-shirt, it didn't show off her assets when she bent over.

Yeah, this would definitely work.

Dropping the towel in the hamper in the bathroom, and the T-shirt off in the guest bedroom for later, she walked into the kitchen. Rodeo was parked beside the island while Jax was standing barefoot at the stove wearing a T-shirt and a pair of jogging shorts that showed off his sexy muscles as he cooked scrambled eggs. She was still appreciating his well-sculpted biceps when she realized he'd made small breakfast steaks and toast to go with the aforementioned eggs.

Skye was about to point out that it was four o'clock in the morning and that he didn't have to go to all that trouble. She would have been fine with a handful of chips or cookies, or even a sandwich. But then Jax turned to look at her, and she forgot what she was going to say.

He took in the dress shirt she wore, his gaze lingering on her bare legs. Something that looked like hunger flared in his dark eyes, but he turned back to the stove before she could be sure.

"Have a seat," he said over his shoulder. "The eggs are almost done."

She turned to the table to find it set with silverware and tall glasses of orange juice. No coffee, though. Which was probably a good thing if either of them planned on getting any sleep this morning. She sat down and reached for her glass just as Jax came over with two plates of food.

"You didn't have to go to the trouble of all this," she said as he sat down across from her. "I would have been happy with a snack."

He shook his head. "It wasn't any trouble. I usually make something to eat when I get home from my shift anyway."

Somehow, she doubted he bothered grilling steak and making scrambled eggs every day. "Well, thank you."

Picking up her knife, Skye spread butter on her toast, then added a generous amount of orange marmalade before taking a bite. *Mmm*. She never remembered a simple piece of buttered toast tasting this good. The steak and eggs were even better. She must be hungrier than she realized. Or it could simply be that Jax was such a good cook. Then again, he was a firefighter. Knowing how to cook was part of the job description.

"How have you been?" Jax glanced at her as he pushed eggs onto his fork with the edge of his toast, then softly added, "Since your parents passed away, I mean. I know the fire at the hotel must have brought up bad memories for you."

The toast she'd been chewing suddenly went dry in her mouth and Skye took a sip of juice to wash it down. After ten years, the memory should have dimmed. But it hadn't. And after tonight, it was even more vivid.

She'd been halfway through her sophomore year in high school when their house caught fire. She'd been at a movie with friends and gotten back just in time to watch

34

her childhood home go up in flames. Dane had tried to save their mom and dad, but hadn't been able to get them out. He'd barely made it out alive himself. She didn't even want to think how close she'd almost come to losing her brother that night, too.

"I'm okay," she said quietly. "It was a long time ago. At least I can talk about it without breaking down and crying anymore."

"There's no shame in crying." He regarded her with sad eyes, then cleared his throat. "I'm sorry I wasn't here for you and Dane. By the time I got back into town, you'd already graduated from high school and headed off to college."

She used what was left of her toast to chase a piece of egg onto her fork and chewed slowly. "I hated leaving Dane, but he insisted it was what Mom and Dad would have wanted, so I went."

Her brother had planned to go to college, too, but he'd put that on hold to pay for her schooling. By the time she'd finished and paid him back, he seemed to have lost interest. He'd never admitted it, but sometimes she wondered if he blamed her for making him give it up. It would certainly explain why he hadn't ever wanted her to come home on vacation.

"You went to college for economics, right?" Jax asked.

She nodded. "I originally planned to go to school for something creative, like graphic art or interior design, but Dad was an economics teacher, and always wanted me to go into math or finances. So I ended up majoring in economics with minors in finance, accounting, and business statistics."

Across from her, Jax's eyes looked like they were about to glaze over. "Wow. That sounds…"

"Boring as hell?" she finished.

"I wasn't going to say that."

She laughed. "Yes you were and you know it. And you're right. It *was* boring. I might be good at math, but I don't love it the way my dad did. Taking all those classes didn't give me much time to think about anything else, though, and back then, that was a good thing. And as an added bonus, I landed an amazing job when I graduated."

Jax studied her, his dark eyes thoughtful. "If it was such an amazing job, why did you quit?"

She shrugged and looked down at her nearly empty plate. "I took a look at my life and realized I'd been living it for other people for so long that I'd stopped living it for me."

"By 'other people,' you mean your parents?"

"Mostly them, yeah, but Dane, too." She chewed on her lower lip. "There was also my ex-boyfriend, Jordan. We'd been dating for a while and it occurred to me that he was making all these plans for me without even asking if any of it was what I wanted. He was setting a wedding date before we even talked about getting married. He had a five-year plan that included everything from when we would have kids and how many we would have, to what social circles I needed to be part of so he could become a partner in his law firm."

Jax snorted. "He sounds like a jackass."

"He is," she agreed. "I'm just sorry it took me so long to see it. I'd probably still be back in New York clueless if it wasn't for Jordan's best friend, Aiden. He convinced me I need to figure out what I want to do with my life, then get out there and do it."

"Let's hear it for Aiden then," Jax said.

"Definitely." She smiled. The only thing she'd miss about New York was not getting to hang out with Aiden anymore. "The next day I broke up with Jordan, quit my job, and cashed out my investment portfolio, then booked the first flight to Dallas."

"Wow." Jax lifted a brow. "Okay, some people might say that's a bit abrupt. But instead I'll just applaud you for your decisive decision-making skills. So, what kind of business are you going to start?"

Skye finished the last of her eggs and set her knife and fork on the empty plate. "A bakery called Comfort Cakes. I plan on focusing on the internet market and special events, like weddings, conferences, and conventions to start with. Then after I get established, I can get a storefront and grow into a full-service dessert catering business."

She finished in a rush, waiting for Jax to say she was crazy for giving up a six-figure job to open a bakery, but he just nodded and polished off the rest of his toast.

"Why a bakery?" he asked when he finished chewing.

She shrugged. "I used to spend a lot of time helping Mom bake when I was little. She loved being in the kitchen and showing her affection for people through her food. After my parents passed away, I made cupcakes and gave them to people for all the kind words, cards, and stuff they did for Dane and me. I didn't realize it until much later that I was also doing it because it made me feel better."

Across from her, Jax swigged his orange juice, but didn't say anything.

"I continued baking in college, then as a form of stress relief after I moved to New York," she continued. "Before I knew it, I was staying up late every night making dozens of cupcakes and selling them to people at work and in my apartment building. Even a few wedding planners. It was hard work and didn't pay nearly as well as my day job, but I loved doing it. Baking brought back all the warm, wonderful memories I had of my mom, memories I'd buried away and forgotten. So when Aiden asked me what I wanted to be doing five years from now, I knew I'd rather stay home and bake than go to work on Wall Street."

It felt so good to finally be able to open up and talk about this to someone. And Jax was a damn good listener. He sat across from her, nodding and asking her serious questions as she told him about her dream business and her business plan. It was like he really got it. He even told her that she could stay at his place as long as she needed so she could save money. Even if she didn't hold him to that promise—he was a friend and living here rent free would start wearing on that friendship soon enough—she still appreciated the offer. There weren't many guys like Jax Malloy out there.

It wasn't until they were cleaning up the kitchen and the conversation started to slow that Skye realized they'd been talking for almost three hours.

"I should probably try to grab a few hours of sleep before I go back into work," Jax said as he closed the dishwasher and turned it on.

Skye was having so much fun, she would gladly have stayed up all night, but the sun would be coming up soon and she didn't want Jax going to work exhausted. "Yeah, me too."

She waited while Jax made sure the door was locked and turned out the lights, then together they walked down the hallway to the bedrooms, Rodeo leading the way. When they reached hers, she turned to look at him.

"I really do appreciate you letting me stay here," she said. "I know you don't think it's a big deal, but to me, it is. So, thanks."

"You're welcome." He gave her a small smile. "I know you feel like you're alone right now, but you're not. Promise me that if you need anything, you'll let me know. Okay?"

Tears clogged her throat. She continued to be blown away by how amazing this guy in front of her really was. Giving in to an irresistible urge, she stepped forward and wrapped her arms around him, squeezing him tightly. She'd meant the gesture to be innocent and platonic, but she couldn't miss how broad his chest was and how good it felt to press her breasts against all that solid muscle. She almost moaned when her nipples began to stiffen into firm, sensitive peaks.

Maybe it was just a reaction to her near-death experience, or maybe she was responding this way because she had a crush on Jax for so long. Either way, the smart thing would have been to pull back before he felt the hard pebbles of her nipples through both of their shirts and realize she was getting excited. But her head didn't seem interested in doing the smart thing. If anything, it was urging her to press up against him even more tightly.

Fortunately, she got it together before she embarrassed herself. But right before she dropped her arms and stepped back, she could have sworn she felt something hard and interesting poking her in the tummy. She supposed it could have been his belt—if he'd been wearing one. Clearly, she hadn't been the only one getting a little turned on from a little hug. And for some silly reason, that made her extremely happy.

Jax didn't say anything, but his dark, smoldering eyes practically undressed her where she stood. Skye wet her lips, wondering if he'd kiss her. Or maybe she was the one who'd do the kissing. Because right then, she wouldn't have been surprised if either of those things happened.

But after a long, heart-stopping moment, Jax stepped back. "Good night, Skye," he murmured. "Sleep well. And feel free to make yourself at home while you're here."

Giving her a smile, he turned and walked down the hall, Rodeo at his heels. She waited until he disappeared inside his bedroom before going into her own. She leaned against the door until her pulse returned to something close to normal, then walked over to the bed. She unbuttoned her shirt as she went, her breath hitching as the material grazed her hypersensitive nipples. Draping the dress shirt over the end of the bed, she picked up the long T-shirt she'd left there earlier and pulled it over her head, luxuriating in its softness as she turned out the light and climbed under the covers.

But instead of falling asleep, she lay there in the dark. Between her aroused nipples and the thought of Jax just down the hallway with a hard-on in his shorts—if he even wore shorts when he slept—she was pretty sure sleep was going to be a long time coming.

Sighing, she rolled over on her back and relived the day she'd had. Not the bad parts, but the good stuff. Like running into Jax after all these years and having him offer her a place to stay, not to mention finally having a sounding board she could talk to about following her dreams.

While Aiden Dunn was a good friend, he wasn't Jax. Maybe it was because she'd known Jax since they were kids, but he made her really believe she could start a whole new business from scratch with little more than a hope, a dream, a Kitchen-Aid, and a cupcake pan. It wouldn't be easy, and she was going to have to deal with Dane's disapproval, but with Jax in her corner—symbolically at least— there was nothing she couldn't do.

Chapter Four

JAX YAWNED AS he walked through the station's big roll-up doors. He'd only gotten a couple hours sleep before coming in, but his normal twenty-four hour shift ran until noon, and he felt bad leaving his guys one man short even for as long as he had. He made his way around the side of the sparkling clean fire engine, intending to go to the captain's office when he ran into Dane rounding the back of the truck.

Dane pulled up with a look of surprise—an expression that lasted all of half a second. Eyes narrowing, he glanced behind Jax, then pinned him with a glare.

"Where's my sister?" he demanded.

Shit. Dane might be his best friend, but the guy had one hell of a short fuse, and he'd always been prickly when it came to his sister. Jax certainly understood why. Skye was the only family he had left. But man, right then, his friend was way out of line.

"She's at my place, sleeping in the guest room. She was so exhausted after last night, I wouldn't be surprised if she spends the whole day in bed."

Dane looked concerned for another half second, then he squared his shoulders. "Did she seriously quit her job in New York to come back here? What the hell kind of business is she talking about starting anyway?"

It would have been easier to tell Dane everything, but he couldn't do that. Skye had told him what she had in confidence, believing he wouldn't go running off to tell Dane.

"Skye asked me to not say anything about it to anyone," he said.

"I'm not anyone," Dane ground out. "I'm her brother."

Jax swore silently. Dane was her brother, but he could also be a jackass sometimes—like now. "She'll tell you when she's ready, okay? You just have to be patient."

The muscle in Dane's jaw flexed. *Shit.* Maybe telling him to be patient had been a bad idea. Dane wasn't known for that trait.

"What the hell does that mean?" His friend took a step closer, his fists clenched at his side. "You haven't seen my sister in a decade and all of a sudden you decide you know more about what she needs than I do?"

Now it was Jax's turn to get pissed. "Maybe I do. I haven't seen her in nearly a decade, but how many times have you?"

He knew it was a dirty shot. Dane had told him more than once it bothered him that he and Skye hadn't seen each other more than a couple times since she had left for college. But that didn't keep Jax from taking advantage of Dane's stunned silence.

"Look, your sister is fine," Jax said as calmly as he could. "But she needs you to give her some space."

"You don't need to tell me how to handle my sister," Dane shot back. "I raised her just fine after our parents died."

"Raised her?" Jax snorted. "She's your sister, Dane, not a farm animal! You didn't raise her. She raised herself."

Dane charged him, his fist swinging at the same time. Jax loved Dane like a brother, but he sure as hell wasn't going to be his punching bag. Jax ducked to one side, allowing Dane's fist to slip past him before lunging forward and wrapping his arms around his friend, slamming him sideways into the fire engine.

Dane twisted in Jax's arms, swinging his elbows in an effort to take off his head, cussing the whole time. Jax cussed right back. He was gonna have to deck his friend to end this, and preferably before Dane decked him.

"What the hell is going on out here?" A sharp voice demanded from the back of the station. "You two get paid to fight fires, not each other!"

Jax and Dane immediately broke apart to see their captain coming toward them. Earl Stewart, the senior man in the station, was hard, whipcord lean, and not someone to mince words. He'd run this station for over ten years and didn't put up with things not being done his way. And he sure as hell didn't put up with his people taking shots at each other.

Stewart gave Jax a hard look before turning his gaze on Dane. "I thought you were supposed to be inspecting the SCBA bottles for the next shift, Chandler."

Dane shot Jax a glare that could melt paint off a fire engine, then gave Stewart a nod. "I'm on it now, Captain."

Jax watched him go. Something told him this wasn't going to be the last time he and Dane argued.

He turned back to the station boss, prepared to apologize for the scuffle, but Stewart cut him off. "In my office. Now."

Jax clenched his jaw as he followed the older man, but didn't say anything. He'd already been MIA for a good part of his shift, and that brawl with Dane wasn't going to win him any points.

"I know I missed eight hours of my shift, Captain," he said once the door to the office was closed and they'd both taken a seat—the captain behind his big, dark maple desk. "I'll work today's shift—all twenty-four hours—to make up for the time I took last night."

Stewart scowled. "I don't give a shit about that. You work more hours off the books than anyone in here. I want to know why Dane was trying to smash your face in. I thought you two were friends. Is this about you pulling his sister out of that hotel fire?"

Jax leaned back in his chair with a sigh, not surprised Lieutenant Boone had told the captain about that. Unlike in the movies, firefighters didn't pull people they knew personally out of burning buildings that often.

"It's not so much that I pulled her out of the hotel fire," Jax said. "It's that she was in the hotel in the first place, that she didn't call him when she got into town, and that she decided she'd rather stay with me than her brother."

Stewart lifted a brow. "Ouch. I take it there's some kind of argument going between Dane and Skye, and that neither one of them intend to back down. How did you get yourself in the middle of it?"

Jax frowned. "You know Skye?"

Captain Stewart knew all his people and their immediate families, but Skye had lived up in New York for the past ten years and as far as Jax knew, she'd never stepped foot in the station.

Stewart nodded. "I knew her parents. Went to school with her dad, in fact. They were good people. I was on the truck that rolled to their house the night of the fire, and seeing Dane and Skye like that afterward... Well, it was tough. I knew I couldn't ever take their pain away, but I did what I could. Got Dane into the department. Helped him pick out a college for Skye." He blinked, and for a moment, Jax was sure he caught sight of tears misting the older man's eyes. But they were gone before he could be sure. "So, did Skye and Dane have a fight?"

Jax hadn't known Stewart was friends with the Chandlers. How could he know? Dane never talked about his mom and dad. Ever.

"Yeah," Jax said. "She quit her job in New York to move back here to start a business of her own—one she doesn't think Dane will approve of."

"She's probably right about that," Stewart said. "Dane's a good man, but he has a blind spot when it comes to that sister of his."

Jax couldn't argue. "That's why she was staying at a hotel. She wanted to get her business up and running before Dane knew she was back."

Stewart scowled. "And he got pissed because you offered to let her stay with you?"

"That's part of it," Jax said. "But mostly he got pissed when I wouldn't tell him why Skye quit her job or what kind of business she's starting."

The captain eyed him appraisingly. "You plan on helping Skye, even if it gets you into hot water with Dane?"

Jax shrugged. "Skye could use a friend right now, and since I wasn't around right after her parents died, I figure I owe her. Dane's a big boy. He's just going to have to deal with it."

Stewart was silent for a moment. "Don't worry about finishing the rest of your shift. I'll cover for you. And stay on your normal forty-eight-hour-off routine. If you need any more time off to help Skye get her feet under her, let me know. Normally, I'd expect Dane to take care of this, but right now he's too wrapped up in his own issues to see what his sister really needs."

Jax breathed a sigh of relief. He'd been secretly hoping that was what the captain would say. Now he had more than two days off to focus completely on helping Skye. He couldn't ask for more than that. He thanked his boss and got up to leave, but then stopped.

"I forgot to ask. Did they get everyone out of the hotel okay?"

Stewart nodded. "Looks that way, though it was damn close. Tory did one hell of a job. Probably going to get a commendation out of it."

Jax nodded. He was glad Tory and the others had gotten everyone out. And even more glad Tory was being recognized for it. The guy was a damn fine firefighter, one of the best.

Jax started for the door again, but this time it was the captain who stopped him.

"I thought you'd want to know," he said. "The department is officially calling the fire in the hotel suspicious pending a formal arson investigation. The clean-up crew from Station 15 found evidence of accelerant in a first floor storage space. Probably just some moron leaving a can of gas on the shelf, but you and I both know you can't be too careful."

Jax swore under his breath. That's all the city of Dallas needed, some kind of psycho out there trying to burn down hotels.

* * * * *

Jax expected to find Skye all snuggled up and sleeping in the guest room when he got home, but instead, she was sitting at the kitchen table with his laptop in front of her, wearing a pair of his workout pants, a T-shirt, and the flip-flops he wore when he was too lazy to put on real shoes. Everything was about a dozen sizes too big for her—especially the flip-flops—but damn, did she make it look good.

Rodeo was sleeping on the floor at her feet, but while he lifted his head from his paws, he didn't get up. Skye, on the other hand, didn't notice him standing there at all because she was busy scribbling notes on a pad of paper. He leaned one shoulder against the square pillar between the open-concept kitchen/living room combo and watched her work. The sun coming through the window was like a halo around her, making her look like an angel and taking his breath away.

When she finally looked up and saw him, the smile she gave him almost made his knees weak. If he wasn't leaning against something, he probably would have fallen over.

"I didn't hear you come in," she said.

He pushed himself away from the pillar, praying his legs would support him. "I didn't want to disturb you."

She gestured with her pen. "I was just writing down some ideas. Hope you don't mind that I borrowed your clothes. I tried to wash mine, but after three times through the machine, they still smelled like smoke. Hope you're okay with me using your laptop, too."

He pulled out the chair beside her and sat down. "Of course. I told you to make yourself at home, and I meant it. I'm surprised you got into my computer without the password, though."

She raised an eyebrow. "You do know that having the word *Password* as your password is a really bad idea, right?"

He shrugged. "Anything more complicated and I'd have to put it on a piece of paper and pin it to my fridge. And that wouldn't be any better."

She laughed. "Probably not."

He leaned closer. "So, what are you looking at? Pinterest or something?"

He'd never actually been on Pinterest himself, but he'd had an ex-girlfriend who was addicted to it.

Skye shook her head as she turned her attention back to the screen. "No. I love me some Pinterest, but I can't let myself get distracted right now. I have a meeting with a loan officer from the bank in a couple days and want to make sure my business plan is ready to go."

"Business plan?" He frowned. "I thought you lost your laptop and everything else in the fire."

She glanced at him out of the corner of her eye. "I did, but I keep all my important stuff backed up on the Cloud for just that reason. You do that too, right?"

"Afraid not." He gave her a sheepish smile. "Not just because I don't have anything important enough to back up, but because I don't have a clue what the Cloud is and how to put anything there."

She laughed, and it was a completely beautiful sound. The fact that she could still laugh after the fire and the fight with her brother was amazing.

"So, what's a business plan?" he asked.

Skye scooted her chair closer to his, turning the laptop so he could see the screen, too. "A business plan lays out everything an investor might want to know about my business—my product line, who my customers are going to be, my pricing list, earning versus profit, equipment expenses, rental costs, promotion, and overhead. It shows the investor—in this case, the bank—that I know what I'm doing and have a good chance of being successful."

Jax studied the mountains of information. It definitely seemed like Skye knew what she was talking about. Her plan even showed that she had enough money of her own to spend the first two years growing her client list. He didn't have much money in the bank, but if she'd let him, he'd invest in her.

"You seem to have a pretty good amount of cash set aside," he pointed out. "Why do you even need a loan from the bank?"

"I could go out on my own right now, but that would cut into my long-term reserves, putting my plan at risk," she explained. "My biggest initial cost is getting access to a place to do all my baking. I obviously can't afford my own shop right now, which means sharing space at night in an established baking business. If I can get the bank to give me a loan, I can sign a lease with a place, which will give me priority access at a reduced rent. Plus, I want to show the loan officer my long-term plan for purchasing my own space and see what they think of the idea." She scrolled down the screen. "This part of the plan is where I show them how my expenses would go down once I move to a permanent location."

She scrolled again, showing him what kind of promotion she intended to do, how many baking assistants she'd need, and the costs associated with storefront locations. Damn, she had this well thought out.

"This is really impressive," he said. "When do you meet with the loan officer?"

"I have an appointment Friday at two."

He eyed the laptop screen. "I probably can't ask all the thorny questions they will, but would you like to go through your proposal with me? Sort of a dry run?"

She beamed at him, her blue eyes sparkling. "That's a great idea. Though, could you do me a favor and envision me in a power outfit instead of these sweats?"

He chuckled. "I can do that."

And the image that came to mind was sexy as hell, right down to the sky-high heels he pictured her wearing. Although he had to admit, any intelligent person would be mesmerized by Skye, even if she was wearing baggy sweats.

* * * * *

After the second time through her proposal, during which she kicked off the leather flip-flops she'd borrowed from Jax's closet, Skye decided it was probably time to get out of his place and buy some clothes. She loved wearing his stuff, but she needed to replace her wardrobe if she ever hoped to be ready for her meeting at the bank. Since she didn't know many men who liked shopping, she was surprised when Jax offered to take her to the mall. She fully expected him to hand her the keys to his truck and tell her to have fun.

"I just need to check on the horses before we go," he said.

Skye waited in the kitchen while Jax changed out of his work uniform and into a button-down shirt, a pair of jeans, and cowboy boots. He looked even better in them than she imagined—and she had a pretty vivid imagination.

"What's in there?" she asked, pointing at the smaller structure that stood halfway between the horse barn and the partially open-sided hay storage unit as they walked across the clearing.

"The tractor and lawn mower, as well as tools and all the other stuff I need to keep this place up and running."

The moment Jax led her into the big barn, she picked up the rich scent of horses, hay, and manure. It had been a long time since she'd been around the pleasant smells of a ranch and they immediately took her back to her days as a teenager when hanging out with her friends and having a good time was all that mattered to her. It seemed so long ago, she barely remembered that time in her life.

Skye shook off the bad memories and fell into step beside Jax. The inside of the barn was mostly taken up with the horse stalls, but beyond those, there were two store rooms at the far end for riding tack, feed, and other supplies. A set of double doors covered the back wall. All the stalls were empty except for four of them, two on either side of the wide, central corridor.

"Where are all the other horses?" she asked.

"Out in the pasture. My ranch hands come in early and let them out. But these two," he gestured first to one horse on the left, then one on the right, "have some health issues that I've been keeping an eye on, so they have to stay in for a while. The other two are their best friends, so I let them stay in here with them."

Skye couldn't help smiling at the thought of horses having best friends. How cute was that? She stepped closer to the first pair of horses he'd mentioned to get a better look. She didn't see anything wrong with them. Then again, she really didn't know what she was looking for. While she loved horses, her experience with them was limited to going riding on a friend's ranch when she was sixteen.

"They're so beautiful," she murmured. "Are they going to be okay?"

"Yeah, they'll be fine. Nothing serious."

Jax unlatched the door on the first stall and walked in, attaching a lead line to the big black stallion's halter and leading him out.

"This is Big Joe," he said, patting the horse affectionately on the shoulder. "He tends to get a little frisky with the mares. Don't you, boy?" When the horse snorted in answer Jax gave Skye a wry smile. "Big Joe got himself kicked in the leg the other day by a mare who thought he was getting a little too fresh."

As Jax brought Big Joe out into the main corridor and attached him to an eye hook in the wall, Skye saw the big horseshoe-shaped wound on the upper part of the stallion's right rear leg. It was scarring over, but still looked painful to her.

Jax filled a plastic bucket with water and added some kind of green goo to it, then gently began to wash Big Joe's wound.

"This would have healed up two weeks ago, but Joe also likes to roll around in the mud," he said as he dipped the sponge in the water again. "He just about got the wound infected, too, which is why he's grounded in his stall now. Another two weeks and he should be fine."

Skye ran her hand down the horse's strong neck, feeling a little tug on her heart as she watched Jax carefully tend to Big Joe. It was clear to anyone that he adored these horses, and since she was a huge animal lover herself, that made Jax even more attractive in her opinion.

As he worked, they talked about the time and commitment it took to keep a ranch like his up and running. In addition to taking care of the horses and the small herd of cows he had, he also had to maintain the barns and outbuildings. But even though it seemed like another full-time job in addition to the one he had at the fire department, she could tell from the way he talked about the place that he loved it.

"I think I spent more time here as a kid than I did at home." He tossed the sponge in the bucket and grabbed a towel from the shelf, then tenderly wiped down Big Joe's flank. "I have so many happy memories associated with this place that I knew I could never sell it when my grandparents passed away and left it to me, no matter how much hard work it took to keep it going."

He finished up with Big Joe and led him back into his stall, then moved to the next one. The chestnut mare inside regarded Big Joe for a moment before coming over to greet Jax.

"This is Star," he said as he ran his hand down the horse's rich, brown coat. "She and Big Joe have this love/hate relationship going on. He loves her, but she hates that he loves all the other mares, too. She's the one who thumped him in the leg. I think she was probably aiming for his ass."

Skye laughed as she caressed the mare.

"Here."

Jax handed her a nugget-shaped treat for her to give Star, then offered one to Big Joe before walking over to the stalls across from her. Skye's hand stilled on the mare's neck, her eyes going wide as he opened the gate and led out a dappled gray mare. The horse's belly was absolutely huge.

"Don't tell me this is one of Big Joe's conquests!" she said.

Jax chuckled as he snapped the horse into the same eyehook Big Joe had been attached to. "No. Lulu's heart belongs to Ghost." He motioned toward the regal looking white stallion in the stall beside the pregnant mare. "But she's getting close to giving birth, so I've been keeping her inside."

Skye slowly moved closer, not wanting to spook Lulu as Jax examined the horse. She smiled as he murmured soft words of assurance to the mare.

"You were absolutely born to do this, weren't you?" she said.

Jax's mouth edged up. "Probably."

"If you love ranching so much, why become a firefighter? It has to be difficult to do both jobs," she observed.

He caressed Lulu's nose with a shrug. "I'd just run the ranch if I could, but I need a steady paycheck to help me cover the cost of this place. I enjoy being a firefighter, too, so it works out well."

Skye took one of the grooming brushes off the shelf and gently ran it down Lulu's back. Even though she hadn't been around horses in over a decade, the move came naturally, reminding her again how much she'd missed home.

She glanced at Jax. "How did you go from working on oil rigs to becoming a firefighter anyway?"

"I came back to Dallas when my grandparents passed away to find out that they'd left me the ranch. I think it was their way of getting me to come back home and settle down," he said, glancing at her over Lulu's back. "It worked, too, much to my mom and dad's delight. I didn't have the heart to go back to working on oil rigs and let someone else run the place. That said, I also knew I could never afford to keep it without a steady job. That's when Dane mentioned the fire department was looking for people. I gave it a shot and never looked back." He shrugged. "Like I said—I enjoy the work, I'm good at it, and it gives me a chance to work with Dane, who, when he's not being a butthead, is my best friend."

Taking Lulu's lead line, he walked her back over to her stall, then gave her some extra hay to munch before securing the latch on the door.

Skye wandered over to Ghost's stall to give him a pat on the neck. Up close, he was even more magnificent. "It's been so long since I've been around horses that I forgot how amazing they are."

Jax came to stand beside her. "You want to go for a ride before we hit the mall?"

Skye's first instinct was to say yes, but she quickly caught herself. She hadn't ridden on a horse in a long time and wasn't sure she was confident enough to jump on one just like that.

"That's no problem," Jax said when she told him as much. "We can ride together."

As in her sitting in front of him with his arms around her? What woman could pass up an offer like that?

She smiled. "Okay. If you're sure you don't mind."

But Jax was already leading Ghost out of his stall and saddling him up with smooth, experienced hands. When he was done, he turned and held out his hand.

"Ladies first."

Pulse skipping a little, Skye kicked off her flip-flops and took his hand, letting him help her up into the saddle. Jax swung up effortlessly behind her, then took the reins and gently nudged the big horse in the ribs. A moment later, they were trotting out of the barn and into the pasture.

She hadn't ever ridden with a guy like this, but she had to admit that sharing a saddle with him was very sexy. She loved leaning back against the solid wall of muscle that was his chest, and the way his strong arms wrapped around her so he could hold the reins, but she loved the way her ass snuggled up against his blue-jean-covered hard-on even more. And there was no mistaking that he was at least semi-erect. She bounced up and down against his shaft with every trot. Between his cock rubbing against her butt and the saddle horn pressing against her pussy, she had to catch her lip between her teeth to stifle a moan.

Then there was the fact that she wasn't wearing a bra. While she wasn't well-endowed compared to a supermodel, there was some serious jiggling going on which made her breasts practically bounce against his biceps. Her nipples tingled so much, it was all she could do not to give them a squeeze.

Luckily, Jax kept up a nonstop commentary as they rode, pointing out different projects he was working on and naming the other horses in the pasture that lifted their heads to watch them pass by. It didn't stop her from getting excited, especially when he leaned forward and put his mouth close to her ear when he talked or flexed his muscled thighs against hers as he guided Ghost where he wanted him to go, but at least she had something to focus on other than how wet her panties were getting. She was definitely going to have to wash his workout pants before she gave them back to him.

By the time he guided Ghost back into the barn and helped her out of the saddle, her knees were so weak from being aroused, she had to hold on to a stall door as Jax fed and brushed down the stallion. If their ride had lasted any longer, she probably would have orgasmed right there in Jax's lap. And likely would have fallen off, too. As if coming from a horseback ride wouldn't have been embarrassing enough.

Star and Lulu gave her knowing looks. Like they were saying, "*A good ride will do that every time.*"

Jax closed the door on Ghost's stall, then turned to look at her. "You ready to go?"

More like ready to come, Skye thought. But she probably shouldn't say that out loud. So instead, she smiled and nodded, falling into step beside him as they left the barn.

Thank God Jax didn't realize how turned on she was. That would have been beyond mortifying. She seriously needed to get a grip on herself, and fast. Jax was her brother's friend—and hers. Plus, he was helping her out of a bad situation. She didn't need to complicate things by fantasizing about him like she was some kind of sex crazed nymphomaniac—even if the sight of him did make her melt.

Chapter Five

SKYE HOPED SHOPPING would get her mind off Jax and her body's insane sexual attraction to him. It didn't.

The moment they got to the mall, she had to go straight to the Victoria's Secret store because she couldn't get any other clothes until she had a bra and a fresh pair of panties. She was stripping off the workout pants and T-shirt when it struck her that she was separated from Jax by nothing more than a few feet of distance and a half-door he could easily peek over. Not that he ever would, she was sure. But it was still a turn-on to stand there naked so close to him.

Her clit tingled as she wiggled into the first pair of panties she'd picked out—hipsters with a cute lacy border. She wasn't as in love with the color now that she was wearing them, but she couldn't put them back. They would be a wet mess. She left them on, telling herself she'd grab a few more in other colors. Ignoring the urge to caress her clit, she slipped into the bra and gasped as the silky material came into contact with her nipples. They were so sensitive they hurt.

"You okay in there?" Jax asked from just outside the door, making her jump. "You didn't stick yourself with a needle or anything did you?"

"No, I'm good," she called back. "Just about done."

Fortunately, the bra fit fine, so she didn't have to try on a bunch of different ones. She took off the tags from both the bra and the panties so she could give them to the cashier, then did the same with the pair of Victoria Secret's signature *PINK* boyfriend lounge pants and tee before pulling those on, too. Shoving her feet into the new flip-flops she'd grabbed, she picked up Jax's clothes and the recent additions to her wardrobe and slipped out of the dressing room.

Jax turned to face her, his eyes caressing her in that same way they had last night when she'd walked into his kitchen in nothing but his dress shirt. She stared back, clutching her new undies in one arm and his borrowed clothes in the other, heat pooling between her thighs.

Jax was the first to recover, stepping forward to relieve her of his clothes. "Let me get those. You ready?"

"I just need a few more things," she said.

As he followed her through the store, Skye resisted the urge to look over her shoulder to see if Jax was checking out her ass, which was currently sporting the word *PINK* across it in bright blue letters. She picked out two more bras and half a dozen panties, then headed up to the counter to pay.

Skye thought the cashier would take issue with her wearing half the clothes she was buying, but producing the price tags was good enough for the woman behind the counter. That didn't keep the woman from eyeing them curiously as she rang up Skye's purchases. No doubt trying to figure out what the heck the story was between Skye and the hot cowboy firefighter at her side.

The remainder of the shopping trip wasn't quite so eventful. Skye shopped as quickly as she could, but it still took a few hours to get everything she needed, including a conservative skirt suit set and matching pumps for her meeting at the bank. Jax didn't say anything as he added yet another shopping bag to the bunch in his hand when they walked out of the last store, but she could tell he wasn't a fan of marathon shopping.

Skye spent a good portion of the drive back to Jax's ranch trying to understand why she was so hot for Jax. Having a teenage crush on him might have been part of it. That and the fact that he'd grown into one of the hunkiest guys she'd ever met. It was possible it was also because he was being so nice to her just when she needed it. But seriously, getting wet in the dressing room just because he was on the other side of the door? That was crazy. Even now, sitting in his truck with him, she had to resist the urge to squirm in the seat to ease the throbbing between her legs. She was going to need a cold shower— or two—before having dinner with him tonight or she might jump him before they even finished eating.

But when they pulled up in front of his house, Skye found the perfect thing to crush any arousing thoughts she might be having— Dane. Her brother was leaning back against his truck with a pissed off look on his face.

Jax cut the engine and reached for the door handle. "I'll handle this."

"No," she said quickly. "I appreciate it, I really do, but I have to deal with him at some point. It might as well be now."

Grabbing as many bags as she could carry from the seat beside her, Skye climbed out of the truck and stomped around the front to face her brother. Behind her, she heard Jax's door slam shut.

"Your boyfriend called me," Dane said without preamble, not even bothering to look at Jax. "He said you gave him my phone number for emergencies, and since your number is out of service, he called me. He thinks you've had a nervous breakdown or something—quitting your job and dumping him so you could move back to Dallas to make cupcakes." He swore. "Cupcakes, Skye. Are you fucking serious?"

She tightened her grip on the bags, fighting the urge to smack her brother with them. God, she was so tired of his crap. "Yes, I'm very serious about making cupcakes. And Jordan isn't my boyfriend anymore. The only reason he's upset about me dumping him and moving back here is that he'll finally have to pay someone to manage his investment portfolio instead of having me do it."

Dane snorted. "I wouldn't bet on that. He seemed pretty upset when I told him you were staying with a friend at his ranch. He asked me if you two were an item before you went to New York. He was worried that's why you left him. I told him that was crazy, that there was nothing going on between you and Jax, but after I got off the phone with him, I started thinking maybe he was on to something."

Skye gaped at him. "What the hell is wrong with you? You know Jax and I were never together before I moved to New York."

He shrugged. "Do I? You were crushing on Jax like crazy back when we were in high school. Maybe you two hung out together without me knowing about it. Maybe you came back in between semesters in college to see him. Hell, maybe you two have been sleeping together on and off for the past ten years."

Her face flamed scarlet. She couldn't believe Dane would say something like that in front of Jax. "You're a complete ass, Dane, you know that? I never slept with Jax, not that it's any of your business. "

Unable to even look at him anymore, she turned and stomped toward the house, her flip-flops slapping loudly against her feet.

"You are not staying here tonight, Skye!" Dane shouted.

She whirled around to tell him to go to hell, but Jax beat her to it.

"That's enough, Dane," he said. "Skye wanted me to stay out of this, but I'm not going to stand here and let you treat her like this. Skye can stay wherever the hell she wants. And if she wants to stay here, she's more than welcome."

Skye bit her lip. Dammit. She appreciated that Jax was standing up for her, but she hated coming between them. They'd been friends since they were kids.

"Dane, please—" she began, but her brother cut her off.

"Get the hell out of my way, Jax!" Dane ordered. "This is between my sister and me. It's time she grew up and dealt with life instead of running away from it like she did when she left Dallas. And if I find out I was right about you sleeping with her, I'll kill you!"

Skye might have gasped, but she wasn't sure. Because before the sound left her lips, Dane drew back his fist and threw a punch at

Jax. It clipped Jax on the jaw, but he shook it off and gave as good as he got, his fist snapping out in a jab and catching Dane right on the chin, stunning him and sending him stumbling backward. But her brother was almost as big as Jax, and didn't go down. Instead, Dane snarled in rage and slammed into Jax, driving him to the ground. Jax immediately flipped him, sending Dane rolling across the gravel.

Skye thought that would be the end of it, but Jax and Dane were both on their feet in a flash, looking like they wanted to tear each other to pieces. *Crap*, they weren't going to stop until somebody got hurt. Skye dropped her shopping bags and ran over to them, shoving herself between Jax and her brother, even though that was a damn dangerous place to be at the moment.

"Stop it right now!" she shouted, putting a hand on each of their chests. "Both of you!"

Giving Jax a little shove, she turned to face her brother. Dane looked mad enough to bite through a horseshoe, but that didn't stop her from glaring at him.

"I never ran away from anything, Dane," she said before he could open his mouth. "And I left Dallas because you wanted me to. When Mom and Dad died, you couldn't get me bundled up and out of your hair fast enough. It was like you couldn't stand to look at me."

Dane reeled back as if she'd smacked him, but now that the words were finally coming out, Skye couldn't stop them. "All I wanted to do was stay home and be with the only family I had left. But you decided you knew what was best for me, without ever considering what I might want." She thumped him in the chest, not even trying to hold back the tears or the anger. "I dumped Jordan the moment I realized he was just like you—deciding what kind of life was right for me, telling me where I should go and who to associate with. Well, I wasn't going to put up with that crap from him, and I sure as hell am not going to put up with it from you anymore, either. I'm staying with Jax because he's never once tried to tell me what to do. He supports me and wants what's best for me, as any good friend would, something I never got from you, my own frigging brother!"

Tears running down her face, she turned and marched back to where she'd dropped the shopping bags. It took some doing to get all of them situated on her fingers, but when she did, she turned to glower at her brother.

"And let's get something else straight. When Jax and I sleep together, it sure as hell won't be any of your damn business!"

Tightening her grip on the bags, she dragged them up the steps and into the house, slamming the door behind her as hard as she could. She wanted her brother to know she was done—with the argument and with him. And if that meant she was closing the door on him forever, then so be it.

* * * * *

"I think it's time for you to leave, Dane," Jax said softly.

He'd managed to avoid another run-in with Dane on his way out of the fire station that afternoon, but he should have known his friend would show up sooner or later. His jaw was smarting a little from the glancing blow Dane landed, but he knew Dane had to be hurting more. And not just from that solid jab to the chin Jax had given him, either. The pain in his friend's blue eyes had nothing to do with Jax's punch and everything to do with what Skye had said.

Dane cleared his throat. "Maybe I should try to…"

Jax shook his head. "Not now, Dane. It's too soon. You both need to let some time pass. You can't just talk this out."

Dane hesitated, his gaze going to the house. After a moment, he nodded. "I never wanted to do anything but help Skye. She took Mom and Dad's death really hard. I thought getting her into a good college was the right thing to do."

"I know," Jax said. "And I probably would have done the same thing if I'd been in your place. But Skye wasn't the only one who took your parents' death hard. You did, too. You dealt with it by burying yourself in work, spending every minute of the day trying to make enough money so Skye could go to college." He put a hand on Dane's shoulder, giving him a rough shake. "But burying yourself in work is the way guys deal with things, not women. The way Skye saw it, shipping her off to college was the same as flat out ignoring her."

Dane's shoulders sagged. "That's not what I intended."

"I know, but it's not anything you can fix with a simple apology, at least not right now. It's going to take some time. Look, just go home, okay? I'll call you in a couple days."

Dane looked like Jax had kicked him in the balls instead of punching him in the face. But he nodded and walked back over to his truck. After another quick glance toward the house, he got in and drove away.

Jax watched him go, wondering if the rift between Skye and Dane could ever be fixed. For both their sakes, he hoped so.

Chapter Six

JAX HEARD SKYE crying before he even reached the door to her bedroom. He cringed. God, he hated when women cried. It made him feel completely powerless. And knowing that Skye was the one doing the crying made it even worse. She was more important to him than any woman he'd ever been with. Knowing she was hurting cut him down deep in his soul.

He lifted his hand and knocked softly on the door. "Dane left."

Skye didn't answer.

"He's sorry for all those shitty things he said. He didn't mean any of it."

Still no answer.

Jax knew he should give her some time alone, but he couldn't get his feet to move. He hadn't been there when Skye needed him ten years ago. He wasn't going to do that to her again. So instead, he leaned back against the wall and slowly slid down it until he was sitting on the floor. Then he rested his head back against the wall and his forearms on his knees and listened to her cry.

He wasn't sure how long he sat there before Skye's tears slowed, then eventually stopped altogether. A moment later, she made a little sniffling noise that sounded so damn cute he couldn't help but smile. He was about to rap on the door again when he heard the bed creak as she got up. She didn't open the door right away, though. Maybe she was checking her make-up, or doing whatever strange ritual women did after crying.

A few minutes later, the door opened and she came out. She was still wearing the snug fitting black pants with the flared bottoms and the tee she'd gotten at Victoria's Secret, but had ditched the flip-flops. Her nose was a little rosy and her eyes were red rimmed and a tiny bit puffy, but neither detracted from her natural beauty.

Skye slid down the wall to sit next to him, but didn't say anything.

"So, you had a crush on me in high school, huh?" The words were out before he even knew what he was saying. He cringed inside. But it was better talking about that than bringing up the shitty stuff Dane had said, wasn't it? "Why didn't you ever let me know you were interested?"

She tucked her hair behind her ear and gave him a wry look. "Why didn't I let you know? Because you're almost four years older than I am and if we dated when you were a senior and I was a freshman, it probably would have sent you to jail."

He thought about that, then grinned. "Good point. Thank you for keeping me out of jail."

They sat there in silence for a while, her left knee touching his right one.

"Thanks for sticking up for me with Dane," she said softly. "I'm sorry it got you punched in the face. Does it hurt much?"

"Nah." He reached up and rubbed the side of his jaw to prove his point. It wasn't that bad. God knew, he'd certainly had worse. "Dane hits like a wuss. It won't even leave a bruise."

She frowned, her brows puckering as she studied his face. "I hate that I'm putting you in the middle of this whole thing."

"You didn't put me in the middle of anything, Skye. I chose to be there," Jax said firmly. "Dane knows he's been acting like a jackass. He'll get his head screwed on straight at some point and come back with his hat in his hand."

Skye didn't look like she believed him, but she didn't call him on it. "I'm sorry about the stuff I said out there. About sleeping with you."

Jax had been wondering about the comment she'd thrown out just before storming into the house. He couldn't lie and say he hadn't been thinking about sleeping with Skye, too. It had been the number one thought on his mind since seeing her walk into his kitchen wearing nothing but his dress shirt. And that horse ride they'd taken together earlier had left him as hard as a fence rail. But without knowing how she really felt about him, he sure as hell wouldn't make a move on her.

"Did you mean it?" he asked softly. "Or did you just say that to make your brother mad?"

He was asking not only because he needed to know, but because he wanted to give her a way out if she had simply said it to piss off her brother. He didn't even realize he was holding his breath until she turned those big, blue eyes on him.

"No, I didn't just say it because I was trying to make him mad. I said it because I've been thinking about it ever since you walked into the hospital this morning." She wet her lips, then caught the lower one between her teeth. The sight made his cock stiffen. "Being away for ten years hasn't changed anything. I'm more attracted to you now than I ever was." She gave him a sheepish look. "I hope that doesn't make you uncomfortable."

The only part of him that was fast becoming uncomfortable was his shaft, and that was because it was straining against the front of his jeans. "Not as long as you don't mind me admitting that I've been having some decidedly more-than-friendly thoughts about you since you've gotten back in town."

Her lips curved into a naughty smile. "I don't mind at all."

They sat there gazing at each other, neither of them saying anything, instead letting their eyes do all the talking. And hers were saying a hell of a lot. Finally, unable to take it anymore, Jax leaned forward to kiss her. Skye didn't wait for him to get there, but met him halfway.

Their lips came together in a slow, tender kiss. She tasted like a juicy peach on a hot summer day, and Jax had to force himself not to go too fast. He wanted Skye to make one-hundred percent sure this was really where she wanted their friendship to go. But based on the way she was kissing him back, she wasn't questioning this decision at all.

Jax buried one hand into her long, silky hair, pulling her closer and slipping his tongue into her mouth with a groan. Skye tangled her tongue with his, sliding a hand behind his head and yanking him in tighter. Her other hand eagerly started undoing the buttons of his shirt, and he briefly wondered if they might end up making love right there in the hallway.

But he decided against it. Not that making love to Skye on the floor wouldn't be amazing, but because doing it in bed—at least the first time—would be even better.

He pulled his mouth away and stood up. Taking her hand, he tugged her to her feet and swung her up in his arms. Then he carried her down the hall and into his room.

* * * * *

Skye expected Jax to set her down on her feet, but instead he gently tossed her on the bed. She started to laugh, but it came out sounding more like a moan as he stripped off his shirt. She had to work hard to control herself as she stared at his six-pack. Those abs were enough to make her want to crawl across the bed and worship him. Then he kicked off his boots, unbuckled his belt and dropped his jeans to the floor, and she just about swooned like a heroine out of a romance book. She'd known he had a great body underneath those clothes, but *daaaaammmn*.

His long, erect cock jutted straight out from between his muscular legs, pulsing slightly in time with his heartbeat and already throbbing with need. It had been one thing to feel his hard-on pressing up against her ass as they went horseback riding that morning, but this was so much different.

She rolled over on her stomach and wiggled forward, drawn toward Jax—and his cock—like she was hypnotized. She felt strangely turned on by the fact that she was still completely clothed while Jax was bare-ass naked. Maybe she could have him walk around the house like this all the time.

When she reached the edge of the bed, he moved closer, bringing his beautiful shaft right into alignment with her mouth. What kind of girl could pass up an offer like that?

Not her, that was for sure.

Skye reached out and wrapped her hand around the thick base of his cock tugging him closer. Then she extended her tongue and swiped it across the bead of pre-cum waiting for her at the very tip. It was sweet and just the tiniest bit musky.

"Mmm," she moaned, and Jax mimicked the sound. How was it possible for a man to taste so good?

She wiggled forward a little more, closing her eyes and swirling her tongue around and around the head of his cock like it was a lollipop. Only better. In between, she took him deeper, letting the very tip touch the back of her throat before pulling back to focus on the head again.

Jax's hand came up to cradle the back of her head, his fingers slipping into her hair. He didn't try to take charge, though. If anything, he seemed more interested in slowing her down. She would have laughed—if that was possible with her mouth so full. Not that she would have complied anyway. She intended to keep doing what she was doing until Jax exploded. And from the way his hips began to flex and thrust in time with her licking, it would be soon.

But Jax had other plans, Just when she was sure he was about to come, he tightened his fingers in her hair and slid out of her mouth.

"Hey!" she protested, tilting her head to the side to look up at him. "I had something special in mind for him."

Jax chuckled. "I bet you did. But I have some plans of my own—and they don't involve letting you make me come in the first ten minutes, or you keeping your clothes on."

Skye gave him a pout, but didn't complain. She wanted this to last just as long as he did. And as for her clothes, she was ready for some skin-on-skin contact herself. So when he spun her around on the bed and eagerly stripped off her pants, she lifted her butt off the bed to help. Her tee and bra quickly followed. That left her lying on his bed wearing nothing but her new panties, which had only gotten wet all over again while she'd been licking him.

She quickly reached down to take them off, hoping to keep Jax from seeing what a complete mess she'd made down there, but he wasn't having any of it.

He caught her hand and shook his head. "That's my job, and I take my job very seriously."

The smolder in his dark eyes told her he wasn't teasing about that. Her heart raced as he hooked his fingers in the waistband of her panties and began to slide them down inch by agonizing inch. She blushed as the soaking wet material clung to her pussy for a moment before he pulled it away to leave a trail of clear, gooey liquid along her inner thighs.

He paused with her panties banded around her knees, gliding his fingers up her legs to trace them around her wet pussy, but not touching it. She bit her lip.

"How long have you been aroused?" he asked softly.

She caught her breath at the hunger in his eyes. "Since going riding with you this morning."

He teased his fingers closer to her clit, his sensuous lips curving into a sexy smile. "I guess you must like riding horses, huh?"

Skye opened her mouth to answer, but all she could do was moan as he slid a single finger up and down her folds. With her panties still around her knees, she couldn't open her legs as wide as she'd like to, but she could definitely roll her hips. She was so desperate to feel that finger on her clit, she was almost dizzy.

"It wasn't the ride," she gasped as his fingertip lightly grazed her clit. "It was feeling your hard-on pressing against my ass."

He grinned, placing his fingers in the folds on either side of her pussy and rubbing them up and down. All he'd have to do was slide down a little more and he'd be plunging those fingers inside her.

"So you like the feel of my cock against that beautiful ass of yours, huh?" he said huskily. "That's something I'm going to have to remember."

She closed her eyes, imagining what Jax meant by those naughty words as she let herself enjoy what he was doing with his fingers. She was so caught up in the blissful sensations she didn't realize he'd slipped her panties all the way off until she felt him spread her legs wide and dip his fingers deep inside.

Her eyes shot open, but it was too late to do much more than inhale sharply as Jax brought his thumb up and pressed it rhythmically around in little circles right on her clit at the same time two of his fingers slipped in and out of her pussy.

She writhed on the bed, rotating her hips in a circular motion in time with his movements. She clutched the sheets in one hand and a handful of his hair in the other, holding on for dear life as her body spasmed over and over. Then she let out a little scream as she arched up off the bed and came long and hard.

Skye was just floating back down to earth from the first orgasm she'd had in months—at least one she hadn't given herself—when she felt Jax's weight on the bed. She opened her eyes to see him leaning over her, his body perfectly positioned between her legs. She glanced down and realized he'd slipped a condom over his cock while she'd been recovering from the epic orgasm he'd given her.

She spread her legs wider, wrapping them around his hips and welcoming him in.

Jax didn't tease her, but instead placed the thick head of his shaft against her wet opening and slid all the way in with one long thrust.

She caught her breath as he filled her completely. They couldn't have fit together any better if they'd been made for each other. Or maybe it was because they really *had* been made for each other.

She anchored her heels against his strong, muscular ass and pulled him in even more, making him touch her in places that brought sparkles to her vision.

"You are one amazing, beautiful woman," he whispered in her ear as he slowly began to move inside her. "Do you know that, Skye?"

How was a woman supposed to answer that?

Since she couldn't think of anything witty—not with his cock buried in her like it was—she simply pulled his face around and kissed him long and hard.

She dug her nails into his back and locked her legs around him tighter, doing everything she could think of to urge him to thrust harder. He obeyed her silent command, pounding into her hard enough to take her breath away and make her so lightheaded she thought she might pass out.

But she didn't lose consciousness. Instead, she climbed the slope to another orgasm, one she knew would be better than anything she had ever experienced in her life, when Jax suddenly rolled over, smoothly bringing her around on top of him. The move was so unexpected that all she could do was gasp as she sat there straddling his hips. Then she realized how good it felt to have him inside this way, and she placed her hands on his chest and began riding up and down on his shaft.

Jax cupped her breasts, pinching and rolling her nipples between his fingers until she was sure she would scream. She gyrated on his cock, pressing her clit against him, and moaning and groaning as her climax approached.

The wave arrived in a rush, catching her by surprise. One second it was building higher and higher, the next she was collapsing forward onto his chest and screaming in his ear.

Jax slid his hands down to grab her ass, pulling her onto his hard cock over and over as she closed her eyes and let go of everything holding her down to the ground.

Somewhere in the back of her mind Skye realized Jax was coming with her, but it was impossible to focus on anything right then. She was coming too hard. All she could do was ride out the pleasure.

Afterward, she could only lie there gasping for air against his strong chest, berating herself for not coming back home to Dallas sooner so she and Jax could have been together like this long before now. But as he wrapped his warm, muscular arms around her, she quickly pushed those thoughts away. She was with him now, and that was all that mattered.

* * * * *

"You sure you don't want me to saddle up another horse for you?" Jax asked Skye the next morning. "I have some that are calm enough for you not to have to worry about them trying to buck you off."

Skye shook her head as he helped her up into the saddle in front of him. "No thanks. I prefer to ride with you if you don't mind."

He settled her beautiful ass tightly against his crotch, already feeling his cock harden. "I certainly don't mind, as long as you don't have a problem with something poking you in the bottom."

She flashed him a sexy smile over her shoulder as he trotted Ghost out of the barn and pointed him toward the open pasture. "Why do you think I wanted to ride this way?"

He laughed, a sound quickly cut off by a groan as her butt began to bounce against him, making him even harder. If he didn't know better, he'd think Skye was deliberately pressing back against him in such a way so that her ass was rubbing directly on his cock. Then again, maybe she *was* doing it on purpose.

After spending his days off with Skye, it was going to be tough going back to work tomorrow. He couldn't remember simply hanging out with a woman for so long and enjoying himself so much. Like last night. They'd spent half of it talking about cupcakes and teenage crushes, not to mention making love several more times. And even though it had only been a couple hours since they'd fallen into an exhausted slumber, she seemed like she was ready for more.

Not that he was complaining. Skye was freaking amazing. No woman had ever mesmerized or aroused him like she did, and he counted his lucky stars she'd gotten tired of New York and the high-paying job she'd had and decided to move back to Dallas. If he had his way, Skye was never going to get out of his bed again.

"Do you think it's going to cause problems at work when Dane realizes we're having a relationship?" she asked, leaning back against his chest.

Jax wrapped an arm around her and discovered she'd decided to leave her bra behind in his bedroom. He could tell because her breasts were bouncing sweetly against his forearm as he held her. His cock throbbed a little more in his jeans.

"Dane won't be happy about us being involved, and on a friendship level, it will probably take him a while to get over it," Jax told her. "But from a professional point of view, we'll be fine. He would never let anything affect the way he does the job. He's a good firefighter."

Skye nodded, but didn't say anything. She might be relieved to hear it wouldn't affect their working relationship, but Jax got the feeling she was still worried about what it would do to his friendship with Dane in the long run. Jax would try to repair whatever damage had been done, but he wasn't going to stop seeing Skye simply because her brother didn't like it.

They went for a longer ride today and at a more leisurely pace since they didn't have to go shopping. Jax was extremely grateful for that, especially since he was horny as hell and hard as a rock by the time they got back to the barn.

He dismounted and helped Skye down, but didn't take his hands off her waist right away. The look on her face told him she'd gotten just as turned on from the ride as he had. If he didn't have to unsaddle Ghost and give him a rubdown, he would have swung Skye up in his arms and carried her into the house all the way to his bedroom. But he did have to take care of Ghost.

He gave her a quick kiss on the lips. "I have to give Ghost a rubdown. You can go back to the house if you want. I won't be long."

She smiled. "I'd rather wait here."

While Jax stripped the saddle and tack from Ghost, Skye wandered over to visit with Big Joe, Lulu, and Star. He smiled as he listened to her have an entire conversation with the pregnant mare about whether Lulu had considered baby names yet. He'd had an ex-girlfriend who'd caught him talking to his horses once and actually laughed, saying she thought the idea of having a conversation with any animal was the most stupid thing she'd ever heard. They hadn't dated very long after that.

Jax rubbed Ghost down as quickly as he could, then gave the stallion some fresh hay before latching the stall door. He turned to ask Skye if she was ready to head into the house, but she wrapped her arms around his neck and kissed him before he could. He buried his hand in her hair and kissed her back. He'd never been one to complain about a woman letting him know what she wanted.

Only he didn't know exactly what Skye wanted until she took his hand and led him over to an empty stall. Giving him a naughty smile, she unlatched the door and backed inside, taking him with her. Apparently she couldn't wait until they got to the house. Fine with him.

"Your ranch hands aren't coming today, are they?" she asked.

"They only work when I'm at my day job," he said.

Her smile broadened. "Good."

She undid the buttons on his shirt and pushed it off his shoulders even as he yanked her tank top over her head, exposing her exquisite breasts. He would have pulled her into his arms, but she stopped him, reaching down to undo the buckle on his belt, then the

89

buttons on his 501s. She shoved his jeans down to his thighs before deciding he could handle the rest. While he was taking care of that, she unbuttoned hers and shimmied out of them with more wiggle than any man could ever resist.

He helped her with her panties, sliding them slowly down her thighs, groaning when he saw how wet they were. If she got this excited going horseback riding with him, he'd damn well take her on a ride every morning for the rest of their lives. It wasn't until he stood up and saw her standing completely and gloriously naked before him that he remembered what exactly had gotten her so excited during the ride—his cock rubbing against her ass.

Reaching out, Jax tugged her close for a long, hard kiss, then spun her around and bent her over. Skye took the hint, placing her hands on a bale of hay and stuck her ass out. And God, what an ass it was. Tight, curvy, and so tasty looking it took everything he had not to drop to his knees and start nibbling. Not that he didn't want to nibble, but right then, he had something else in mind. Something he was sure Skye would enjoy.

Placing one hand on her lower back, he lightly trailed his fingers over the curves of her beautiful, heart-shaped bottom. Goose bumps immediately followed wherever he went, and she let out a long, soft moan. He didn't think he'd ever heard a sexier sound.

He trailed his fingers from one cheek to the other, then slightly down into the cleft between them before repeating the move. "Your ass is really sensitive, isn't it?"

She wiggled her ass, trying to keep up with his finger. "I never knew it was, but now that you're touching me, I guess it is."

Jax chuckled softly. He could have some serious fun with an ass as perfect as hers.

But right now wasn't the time for leisurely fun. They were both too excited for that. So he stopped teasing her and cupped one of her ass cheeks in his hand, giving it a firm squeeze.

Skye moaned louder, arching her back and pressing her ass against his hand, silently begging for more. Not wanting to disappoint her, he slipped his other hand between her legs and down to her pussy while he kept massaging her bottom.

She was so wet that his fingers slipped right in, making her jerk and cry out. He thrust with his fingers at the same time he squeezed her bottom, moving in and out with a slow, rhythmic motion. The combination must have really done it for her because she screamed and exploded in orgasm. Damn, she *really* liked having her ass played with. He'd have to definitely remember that.

He scooped up his jeans from where they lay in the hay, digging through the pockets until he found the condom he slipped in there before they'd come out for a ride. He hadn't been sure they'd have sex anywhere but in the house, but like the former Boy Scout he was, he liked to be prepared.

Skye was still leaning against the wall of the stall, her legs quivering as she gasped for breath. Jax rolled on the condom and stepped up behind her. She reared up with a gasp as he grabbed her hips and plunged all the way in with a single hard thrust.

"God yes," she breathed. "Just like that."

He placed his hand on the middle of her back, applying a little pressure and encouraging her to lean over again. She got the message, sticking out her ass and getting a good grip on the bale of hay as he began to pump into her. She was so hot and wet! It was like heaven on earth.

Jax gripped her hips again and thrust faster, his thighs smacking into her ass over and over with a delicious sound. Skye whimpered, shoving her ass back toward him. He lifted his hand and smacked her right cheek.

Skye craned her neck to look at him over her shoulder. "Spank me again."

He complied, bringing his hand down on her left cheek this time. Her ass turned a pretty shade of rose as he spanked her, and the sight of it nearly brought him to his knees.

She arched her back, crying out so loudly that it echoed around the barn. Her pussy tightened and spasmed around his shaft, sending him over the edge. He stopped spanking and gripped her red-hot ass, burying himself all the way inside her and coming so hard his legs practically gave out. The feeling of them both orgasming together, and so perfectly in synch, was unlike anything he'd ever experienced.

When the last of his climax tapered off and he was steady enough to stand, he slid out of Skye's warmth, albeit reluctantly, and pulled her in for a long and lingering kiss. Damn, this was one woman he could get used to being with.

Chapter Seven

JAX PULLED HIS motorcycle into the parking lot of the station house, working hard to wipe what he knew was a silly ass grin off his face. But damn, it was tough. He couldn't remember being this happy in a long time. He only wished there was some way he could have taken today off and spent it with Skye, but he couldn't. The station work schedule had been screwed up enough the last few days.

After that practically transcendent experience in the horse barn followed by a quickie in the shower, he and Skye had gone into the city for her meeting with the loan officer at the bank. While he swigged coffee at the Starbucks next door sweating bullets, worrying about whether she'd get the loan, she'd walked in cool as a cucumber and knocked them dead. The bank had been very receptive to her business plan and was working up a contract for her to look at later in the week.

Afterward, he'd taken her out to dinner to celebrate, then they'd gone back to the ranch to hang out. When Skye had changed out of her suit and into a skimpy pair of shorts and a tank top, he'd been all set to strip them off her, but she'd talked him into helping her make cupcakes instead. Jax wasn't an expert when it came to baking, but he'd helped out as much as he could. He'd made more of a mess than anything else, but Skye didn't seem to mind, especially when he covered her nipples in frosting and licked it off.

He stifled a groan as he parked his bike and cut the engine. Now that image would have him hard all day.

Jax did his best to act like it was just like any other day at work, except for the part where he avoided Dane as much as he could. He was surprisingly successful, mostly since it seemed Dane was trying to do the same thing. They rolled on two traffic accidents and a Dumpster fire, all without saying a word to each other. They even handled the post-response equipment clean-up without any trouble, then dinner later in the day.

But the station was too small to tiptoe around each other forever and after they'd finished eating, Dane cornered him upstairs in the sleeping area, asking him what the hell was going on between Jax and his sister.

Jax clenched his jaw as he stared at the wall above the bed. He thought about lying for a moment, then said screw it. This needed to come out, and now was as good a time as any.

He turned and faced his friend, looking him squarely in the eye. "If you're asking if we're romantically involved, then yeah, we're seeing each other."

Dane's fist clenched at his side, and Jax tensed, ready if his friend started throwing haymakers. But after a long time, Dane just shook his head.

"Dammit Jax, she's my sister."

"I'm well aware of that fact, believe me," Jax said. "But she's also a grown woman who can make decisions for herself."

Dane swore under his breath. "If you hurt her—"

"That's not going to happen," Jax cut him off. "I care about Skye too damn much to ever do something that would hurt her. And you should know that. Shit, Dane, we've been friends since we were five-years-old."

"I know! It's just that…"

Just what? But Dane didn't finish. He didn't try to take a swing at Jax, either, so that was progress at least.

Shaking his head, Dane turned and stomped down the stairs. While their discussion hadn't turned into a fight, Jax didn't feel like lying in bed staring up at the ceiling. And he was too keyed up to read.

He headed back downstairs, but skipped going into the TV room with the rest of the guys, figuring that was where Dane would be. Instead, he slipped outside and called Skye. They'd only slept together two nights and he was already missing her.

"Hey, girl," he said as soon as she picked up. "What are you up to?"

"Jax! Hey!" she said, and all the tension from dealing with Dane's crap disappeared at the sound. "Nothing. I just had something to eat, then went for a walk with Rodeo, and now I'm getting ready for bed."

He wanted to ask if she was wearing one of his dress shirts again, but didn't. He wasn't sure his cock could handle it. He leaned back against the brick wall and steered the conversation toward more work-safe territory. "So, what'd you do today?"

"I spent most of it on the phone, looking for baking shops that would be willing to enter into a long-term lease for use of their equipment. I found two that sound really promising, so I'm going over in the morning to take a look."

At the restaurant last night, they'd talked about what kind of facilities she was looking for, and what she thought it might cost to lease them. But when she told him the kind of money the bakeries were asking, Jax was shocked at how much it cost to rent someone else's mixers, ovens, and bowls.

"Can you still make a profit paying those kind of overhead costs?" he asked.

"It's going to be hard, but I don't really have much choice," she admitted. "It's not like I can make hundreds of cupcakes in your kitchen. It's just not big enough."

"I could install a second oven if it'd help," he offered.

"I appreciate that." He could almost hear her smiling over the phone. "But I don't want to completely take over your life with my baking business. How was your day? Dane wasn't being too much of a pain in the butt, was he?"

"Nah. We actually had a civil conversation a little while ago." He heard a noise in the background that sounded suspiciously like the mattress dipping. "Did you just climb into bed?"

"Yeah. You wore me out last night. I figured I'd go to bed early and catch up on some sleep." Her voice lowered to a throaty purr. "I'd sleep better if you were here, though. It sucks that you have to work twenty-four hour shifts."

"I'm not too thrilled about it either, babe, but you're going to have to get used to it. This is the life of a firefighter—twenty-four hours on, forty-eight off."

"I know, I know." She sighed. "But lying here in bed naked isn't the same without you in it with me."

His cock stirred inside his uniform pants. "You're naked?"

"Yeah." She let out a sexy laugh. "You didn't expect me to put something on just because you're not here, did you?"

Actually, he hadn't thought about it. But now that he was thinking about it, he was rapidly getting hard. "I'm going to have a very difficult time falling asleep tonight, you know that, right?"

She giggled. "Don't you mean you'll have a *hard time* falling asleep?"

Jax groaned and reached down to reposition his hard-on before he hurt himself. "That's exactly what I mean. Good night, Skye."

He stood there waiting for his erection to ease long after she whispered good night in that soft, husky voice of hers and hung up. He seriously doubted he'd be able to fall asleep now, not with thoughts of Skye naked in his bed back at the ranch, but he should at least try. He didn't want to be exhausted when he got off work tomorrow. He had plans for Skye that didn't include sleeping.

Jax headed back inside and was halfway up the steps to the sleeping quarters when the fire bell rang. He turned and ran for the main bay at full speed. Apparently, he wasn't going to be getting any sleep after all.

* * * * *

Jax had just finished eating breakfast the next morning when Captain Stewart called him and the other firefighters into the conference room. He topped off his coffee, then followed Dane and the others in. The captain stood in the front of the room, a grim expression on his face as he waited for them to take their seats.

"I just heard back from the arson division," he said without preamble. "They've confirmed what I thought—that the fire at the hotel on Jacobs Street was deliberate. Investigators found plastic residues from a container of gas in the store room along with cloth fibers from an improvised wick."

Shit. Jax glanced at Dane and saw that his friend was almost certainly thinking the same thing he was. People typically started fires in old buildings or foreclosed properties because they wanted to get out from under them. But if someone started a fire in a hotel full of people, the reason was likely much more sinister.

"Are we looking at a serial pyromaniac here?" a curly-haired firefighter named Glen Bosch asked from the other side of the room.

"That's anyone's guess right now," Stewart said. "This could just be a one-time thing, like some guy looking for revenge against the hotel chain or a disgruntled employee. Or we could be dealing with some kind of psycho who gets off on starting fires. If that's the case, we need to be ready in case he tries to do it again."

His boss probably would have said more, but he was interrupted by the clang of the fire bell. As they raced for the trucks, Jax heard the dispatcher call going out to multiple stations. The fire was at a nearby apartment complex about twenty minutes away. Jax glanced at Dane as they yanked on their turn-out gear. Once again, his friend was wondering the same thing. Was this just a random fire, or another arson attempt?

Jax supposed it didn't really matter. No matter how the fire started, a firefighter had the same job—put it out.

* * * * *

When they arrived on the scene, any thought that the fire was anything other than the work of an arsonist disappeared. The big apartment complex was burning in at least three different places, and that didn't happen on its own. As Jax grabbed his SCBA tank, he overheard Lieutenant Boone talking on the phone with the other responding engines, figuring out who was going to handle which parts of the fire.

Jax quickly headed into the building with Dane and Troy to start getting people out of the two-story structure while the rest of the firefighters got the supply lines attached to the local hydrants and the attack hoses in place to fight the fire.

People were gesturing madly toward the second floor the moment they got inside, shouting that there were several older people who lived up there. Jax and Dane immediately peeled off for the stairs as Tory searched the apartments on the first floor.

The upper floor was a zoo. While some people were running for their lives from the fast growing flames, others seemed more interested in trying to save their TVs and computers. Jax kicked in the first door he found closed and rushed into the apartment to see if anyone was in there.

The fire was eating through the ceiling and covering the walls at a rapid pace, but when he did a quick search, he didn't find anyone. He turned to leave, jerking in surprise as a reflection in the glass of his SCBA facemask caught his attention. He had just a fraction of a second to see a man in a heavy coat and motorcycle helmet swinging something at him. Whatever it was smashed against his fire helmet like a ton of bricks.

Jax went down hard, his vision swimming in a sea of black, gray, and red. He knew even before he hit the floor that he was about to lose consciousness. If he passed out in this fire, he was never going to wake up.

The thought of what Skye would go through when she heard that she'd lost someone else in her life to a fire made him almost as sick as the dizziness overwhelming him.

His hand moved of its own accord to the radio on his belt. There was no way he could call for help, but if he could hit the orange emergency button, it might be even better.

As the unforgiving blackness swooped in and surrounded him, Jax prayed his finger had found that damn little button.

* * * * *

Jax came to as someone pulled him to his feet. A moment later that same someone draped his arm over their shoulder and slowly dragged him along the hallway and over to the stairs. Halfway down the steps, the darkness shrouding his vision finally began to recede. He determinedly got his feet under him and helped whoever was half dragging, half-carrying him by supporting his own weight.

Tory immediately ran over as they came out of the building. Jax waved him off.

"I'm fine," he said.

But Tory ignored him, putting his arm around Jax to support him from the other side. Jax swore and yanked his mask away, shaking them off. "I said I'm fine, dammit! There was someone in that apartment with me. Fucking asshole knocked me out."

Tory stared at him.

"What?" a familiar voice asked from the other side of Jax. He turned to see Dane looking at him like he was crazy.

Jax reached up and pulled off his helmet, turning it around to show Dane and Tory the big dent along one side of it. That would have been his freaking head if he hadn't been wearing a helmet.

"Some asshole in a heavy coat and motorcycle helmet came up behind me and used my head for batting practice. He tried to frigging kill me."

Dane looked at Tory. "Tell the on-scene commander and the cops that someone assaulted a firefighter. Get them looking for this guy." He turned back to Jax. "Come on. Let's get you over to the paramedics."

"I don't need a paramedic," Jax told him. "I'm fine."

"Maybe, but you're getting checked out anyway," Dane said firmly.

Shit, Dane could be stubborn. But unless Jax wanted to go twelve rounds with him in the middle of the parking lot, it was easier to simply let a paramedic take a look at him. The faster he did, the faster he could get back in that building and look for whoever had clocked him.

Unfortunately, a dark-haired female paramedic by the name of Fletcher took one look at his helmet and shoved it into Dane's hands, along with his air bottle and turn-out coat. Then she ordered Jax to sit on the back of an ambulance and shined a penlight in his eyes.

"You aren't going anywhere," she announced.

* * * * *

Skye was bummed to see that the vehicle bay was empty when she pulled into the parking lot of the fire station where Jax worked. After a moment of inspiration involving waffles and bacon, she'd whipped up a batch of cupcakes and brought them in for Jax and the rest of the firefighters to try. It looked like she was going to have to wait until they got back.

She walked into the station and found Captain Stewart and a young female firefighter leaning over the big radio set-up, concern on both their faces. Skye felt a flutter in the pit of her stomach, and immediately tamped it down. Just because they looked worried didn't mean it had anything to do with Jax or her brother.

Her curiosity on the other hand couldn't be so easily ignored. She was just about to ask what was going on, when a burst of chatter came over the station radio. Something about one of the firefighters getting hurt. The flutter in her stomach was back, along with a healthy dose of real fear. Stewart must have heard her gasp because he turned and looked in her direction.

"Skye," he said. "What are you doing here?"

"What happened?" she demanded, ignoring his question. "Who got hurt?"

The older firefighter shook his head. "We're not sure yet. I'm waiting for an official situation report. You can stay, but I need you to be calm. Can you do that?"

Did that mean he'd lied to her about not knowing the identity of the injured firefighter? Was it Jax or Dane?

She wanted to demand that the captain tell her who it was, but was afraid he'd make her leave. So she nodded and stood there numbly as more details began to filter through. They didn't make a lot of sense, though. No one had gotten burned or injured in a fire. Instead, one of them had been assaulted inside a burning apartment building. That couldn't be right. Who would attack a firefighter?

Then she heard the name of the firefighter who'd been attacked.

Jax Malloy.

Skye gripped the edge of the table, afraid her knees were going to give out. The rest of what they said over the radio fell on deaf ears as she started hyperventilating.

Captain Stewart put his arm around her shoulders. "It's all right, Skye. Jax is going to be fine."

Hearing that should have calmed her down, but it wasn't enough to stop her from freaking out. All she could think about was losing Jax. After everything else in her life fire had taken from her, the thought of losing Jax too was just too much to bear.

Captain Stewart said something to the female firefighter, then guided Skye into the vehicle bay.

He led her over to a chair near the wall and gently pushed her down into it, then

106

instructed her to lean over and put her head down. She obeyed, not really sure how it would help. But it did. After a few moments, she didn't feel dizzy anymore. The fear, however, was another matter entirely. It had latched onto her with a viselike grip and refused to let go.

Skye looked at Captain Stewart, searching his lined face. "Is Jax really okay?"

The older man smiled. "He's fine."

She sagged in her chair. "Who would attack a firefighter in a burning building?"

"I don't know. But I sure as hell intend to find out."

Captain Stewart sat with Skye while they waited for the trucks to come back. A rescue vehicle pulled into the station parking lot a little while later followed by two police cruisers. The moment Jax stepped out of the patrol car, she jumped up and ran over to him.

Skye threw her arms around him, smelly fire suit and all. She was so relieved to see him in one piece that she barely paid attention as he explained to the captain about the psycho who'd come at him with a baseball bat in the apartment building. Until he got to the part about Dane coming in to save him. She hadn't even realized her brother had been in the other police car until she finally caught sight of him standing a few feet away.

She let Jax go long enough to rush over to hug Dane. "Thank you for saving Jax."

Dane hugged her back, something he hadn't done in a long time. "Of course I saved him," he said softly into her hair. "Jax might be a jerk, but he's still my friend."

Skye smiled. Maybe Jax and her brother would be able to salvage their relationship after all.

"What happened out there?" Captain Stewart asked.

Skye shuddered as Jax explained how he'd been assaulted and left to burn to death. If her brother hadn't gone looking for him...

"The fire was under control before Jax and I left," Dane added. "The on-scene commander is already calling it arson. With four separate ignition points, there's no way that was an accident."

Captain's Stewart's mouth tightened. "Question is, did the guy assault Jax because he didn't want the fire put out, or did he set the fire so he could lure the fire department there to kill a firefighter?"

Skye felt sick to her stomach at the possibility of either situation. Needing some fresh air, she walked out to the parking lot and over to Jax's truck so she wouldn't have to hear any more.

Jax came out ten minutes later. He took her into his arms and pressed a kiss to her hair.

She closed her eyes and hugged him tightly for a long minute, then pulled back to look up at him. "Are you sure you're really okay?"

He gently ran the backs of his fingers down her cheek. "I'm fine. The paramedic who checked me out said I didn't even have a concussion. And if she was wrong, I know what signs to look for." His mouth quirked. "Besides, my head is too hard for anything to hurt it."

Skye didn't laugh. She didn't think it was funny at all. Jax must have figured that out because he changed the subject.

"You brought cupcakes?"

"What?" She followed his gaze to the Tupperware container in the back seat of his pickup's king cab. "Oh, yeah. I tried a new recipe and thought you and the other firefighters might like them. Waffle flavored cupcakes with maple-bacon frosting."

She opened the door to grab them when one of his fellow firefighters poked his head out of the station telling Jax that the chief was on the line looking for a detailed report on what happened at the apartment building.

"I'll be right in," Jax called over his shoulder. He took the container she offered, holding it in one hand and cupping her face in the other. "I have to go. But I really am fine, okay? I'll be home in a few hours. We can talk as much as you want then."

She nodded. At least he was willing to talk to her about it. A lot of guys wouldn't do that.

He kissed her, then opened the driver's side door. "Drive safe, okay? I'll be home soon."

"I will."

Skye waited while he walked back into the station, waving at him when he lifted a hand in her direction before going back inside. She sighed as she put the truck in gear and pulled out of the parking lot, praying Jax didn't have to go out on another fire before his shift ended. She didn't think he would after getting hurt, but Jax was the type who'd go anyway because he thought it was the right thing to do.

When she got back to the ranch, she played fetch with Rodeo for a while, then puttered around in the kitchen. In theory, she was working on a new cupcake recipe, but mostly she was wasting time until Jax came home. She wasn't sure how they were going to taste since she spent more time worrying about Jax than baking, but she had them out of the oven and just finished frosting them by the time he walked in.

She sagged with relief and dropped the spatula in the empty bowl. She knew she shouldn't still be freaked out, but she couldn't help it. Jax could have been killed today.

That's when it hit her. She was falling hard and fast for Jax.

The realization would have alarmed her if it had been any other guy. But Jax wasn't some guy she'd just met. She'd known him since they were kids. And it wasn't very surprising that her teenage crush had turned into something more now that she'd had a chance to spend some real time with him.

The thought of losing him was what scared her.

Rodeo trotted over to greet Jax, wagging his tail happily. Jax bent to give him a pet and a, "Hey boy," then walked into the kitchen. Rodeo followed at his heels.

"Those smell good," Jax said, glancing at the cupcakes.

She tried to give him a small smile, but couldn't quite manage it. He must have realized she was a mess because he took her hand, then led her to the table and gently pushed her into a chair. Pulling out the one beside her, he sat down and took her hands in his.

"What's going on in your head right now?" he asked. "And don't say nothing because I can see you're upset."

Skye didn't answer right away. She knew she was being unfair. She'd known Jax was a firefighter when she decided to sleep with him. It wasn't his fault that she had a phobia about everything fire related.

"Even though you rescued me from that burning hotel, I let myself forget what you do for a living," she said softly. "Today reminded me in a big, fat way."

"Today was an isolated incident, Skye. I can count on one finger the number of times a guy who set fire to a building hung around and tried to take out a firefighter. I was in more danger when I worked on oil rigs and rode broncs on the rodeo circuit. Hell, I'm in more danger driving to the station."

If he was hoping that would make her feel better, he failed. When she didn't say anything, he let out a heavy sigh.

"It's okay. You don't have to say it. After what happened with your parents, I know how hard it would be for you to be with a guy who goes into burning buildings for a living."

Tears suddenly clogged her throat, and she swallowed hard. He thought she was breaking up with him.

"Jax…"

He brushed her hair back from her face, his dark eyes sad. "Shh. I get it, and it's okay."

But it wasn't okay.

Skye grabbed his hands and held on tightly. "I'm not breaking up with you, Jax. I couldn't even if I wanted to. We have something special, and I'm not going to throw it away just because what you do is dangerous. But I'm not going to ever be cavalier about the risks inherent in your job, either. I don't like fire, and I never will. I'm going to worry about you every time you go to work and there's no getting around that. But I care about you too much to walk away."

Jax sat there for a long time, not saying anything. Then, leaning close, he cupped her face in his hands and kissed her long and hard on the lips.

"Thank you," he whispered when he finally pulled away.

She kissed him again, then tugged him to his feet. She didn't want to talk about fires and burning buildings anymore. "Come on. I tried out a new cupcake recipe and want to know what you think."

Skye waited impatiently while he washed his hands, then peeled off the wrapper and bit into the cupcake. He chewed once, then twice before swallowing and making a face.

"Um, what kind of cupcake is this supposed to be?"

"Pumpkin with cranberry cream cheese frosting." She leaned close and took a bite of the cupcake he was still holding. This time, it was her turn to make a face. She knew she hadn't been paying attention to what she was doing while she was making them, but she'd screwed up the recipe even worse than she thought. "*Ewww*. I think I added way too much nutmeg to the cake and forgot the sugar in the frosting."

Skye took the cupcake from his hand and tossed it in the trash, then dumped the rest of the tray, much to Rodeo's dismay. Giving him a Milk Bone instead, she looked at Jax.

"Want to help me make another batch?" she asked.

His mouth twitched. "Only if I get to lick the frosting off your nipples again."

"Deal." She went up on tiptoe to kiss him. "But only if I get to do the same to you."

She and Jax had just finished frosting the cupcakes when Dane's truck pulled up in front of the ranch house. Luckily, they'd already cleaned up and gotten dressed. Skye groaned as she heard his footsteps on the porch. She really wasn't ready for another argument with her brother.

"If we ignore him, maybe he'll go away," she muttered.

Jax snorted as he walked over to open the door. "You obviously don't know your brother."

Dane strode in, jaw tight. Skye automatically braced herself.

Her brother glanced from her to Jax. "I just got off the phone with the police in New York City. They got my number from a list of emergency numbers your ex-boyfriend has in his apartment."

Skye walked around the island to stand beside Jax. "What were the police doing in Jordan's apartment?"

She was almost afraid to ask. Jordan could be an arrogant jackass sometimes, but he never did anything that would involve the cops.

"One of his neighbors called the police to report a loud argument a few days ago," Dane said. "The police responded and found the place trashed. They're thinking he had a fight with a friend of his named Aiden Dunn."

Skye frowned. "Is he okay?"

Dane shrugged. "Nobody knows. Jordan and Aiden are both missing, but the cops

114

found blood on the floor of your ex's apartment, so they're fearing the worst."

Skye covered her mouth with her hands. "Oh, God."

Jax came over and put his arm around her. "Just because they found blood doesn't mean Aiden's dead."

She nodded. She knew he was right, but she wasn't going to stop worrying until she knew Aiden was safe. If Jordan hurt him—or worse—she'd never forgive her ex.

Dane pulled out his cell phone. "The detective working the case wants you to call and see if you can tell them anything that might help figure out where Aiden and Jordan are."

He scrolled through the numbers in his contact list, then hit one and put the phone on speaker.

"Ansel."

"Detective? This is Dane Chandler. I have my sister Skye with me if you want to talk to her."

"Have you found Aiden and Jordan yet, Detective?" she asked before the cop could say anything.

"Unfortunately, no. We're still looking," Ansel said. "Your brother said you broke up with Jordan McAvoy about a week ago. May I ask why?"

"I finally figured out how manipulating and controlling he was," she said.

"How did he take the break-up?"

"He wasn't happy." Understatement there. "At first, Jordan genuinely seemed hurt when I told him I didn't want to see him anymore. He begged me to stay, and when that didn't work, he got pissed off and told me I'd be sorry I ever left him."

"Did he ever get violent with you?" Ansel asked.

Both Jax and Dane narrowed their eyes at that.

"No. He got angry, but he never got violent," Skye said quickly, answering Ansel's question while reassuring her brother and Jax at the same time. "Do you really think Jordan might have hurt Aiden, Detective?"

Jordan and Aiden had been friends since college. The two of them were so close they should have been pictured next to the word "bromance" in the dictionary. In a way, they'd always reminded her of Jax and Dane. She'd obviously been wrong about that.

"We're not sure, but we're not ruling anything out," was his answer.

Skye was still trying to wrap her head around the idea that her ex-boyfriend may have killed his best friend when Dane spoke.

"Detective Ansel, should we be worried Jordan might come after Skye?"

Skye blinked. "Me?"

Dane slanted her a look. "Jordan obviously has a screw loose. It's not far-fetched to think he might come looking for you."

"Your brother's right, Ms. Chandler," Ansel said. "We don't know what's going on in McAvoy's head. We're checking the airlines, bus stations, and rental car agencies to see if he left the city, but until we know for sure, it's better to keep your eyes open for anything suspicious."

Beside her, Jax frowned. "Detective, this is Jax Malloy. I'm a friend of Skye's. If we're talking about suspicious, we should probably mention someone deliberately set fire to the hotel where she was staying when she first came back to Dallas."

The possibility that her ex-boyfriend might have done such an evil thing was chilling. "You think that was Jordan?"

Jax shrugged. "I don't know. But like Detective Ansel said, we shouldn't rule anything out."

"Which means Jordan might also be the one who assaulted you at that apartment building this morning," Dane added.

Skye swallowed hard. It was bad enough when she thought Jordan might have hurt one of her best friends, but knowing he might have attacked Jax made her feel ill.

"Okay, you lost me," Ansel said over the speaker phone. "Start at the beginning."

Jax explained he was a firefighter along with Dane, then told him about the recent fires and how someone had assaulted him with a baseball bat that morning. If Jax was right about Jordan, that meant he was in as much danger as she was. Had Jordan killed

Aiden because his friend had found out what he was planning? It sounded crazy. And terrifying as hell.

"As soon as I get off the phone with you, I'm going to call down to the Dallas PD with everything we have on McAvoy," Ansel said. "But until they get involved, all of you need to be careful."

"We will," Jax promised.

Dane blew out a breath as he hung up. "Holy crap, Skye. Are we honestly thinking your ex-boyfriend is this arsonist?"

"It fits," Jax said before she could answer. "Skye already said he's controlling and has a temper. It's not too much of a stretch to think he snapped and came down here looking to get back at her."

"And decided to take you out in the process," Dane added.

Skye couldn't believe Jax and her brother were calmly discussing her ex-boyfriend trying to kill her and Jax. And while she didn't want to believe she'd spent the past few years with a man who might be a murderer, even she finally had to agree with their logic. While he hadn't gotten violent with her, Jordan had been furious when she broke things off with him, angrier than she'd ever seen him in fact. What if he'd just snapped? And since her dumbass brother had accidently let slip that she might be sleeping with another man, she had no doubt Jordan would come after Jax, too.

"So what do we do?" she asked.

"Well, for one thing, we call Captain Stewart and let him know what's going on," Jax said. "He can get the DPD involved from this end. If Jordan is the arsonist, hopefully they'll be able to catch him before he sets fire to another building."

Crap, she just thought of something. "Since he set the one this morning to draw you out, I don't think you should be going on any more calls until the cops find him."

Jax cupped her face, his mouth curving. "I can't stay back at the station while everyone else rolls out, Skye. Now that I know there's some guy out there looking to kill me, I'll be ready for him."

Skye opened her mouth to argue, but Dane cut her off.

"The captain will make sure another firefighter is with Jax every time he goes in to put out a fire," her brother promised. "And until they catch Jordan, I'm going to be staying here with you guys."

Jax frowned. "I can protect Skye myself, Dane."

"I didn't say you couldn't. I'll talk to the captain about us alternating duty days too, so that one of us is always with her."

Skye didn't mind the idea of having one of them around 24/7, but she wasn't crazy about Dane staying at the house when Jax was home. She could tell from the look on Jax's face that he wasn't thrilled with the idea, either, but he didn't say anything.

"Do you have a picture of Jordan?" Dane asked Skye as Jax grabbed his cell from the counter and went into the living room to call the captain.

She nodded and opened Jax's laptop, pulling up the photo folder she had on the Cloud. While Dane leaned over her shoulder, she flipped through the pictures until she found one of her, Jordan, and Aiden together at a Yankee's game. She was sitting between the two of them, and all three of them were smiling. Her lips curved as she remembered that day. Looking at her handsome blond-haired ex-boyfriend, it was hard to picture him hurting anyone, much less the boyish Aiden.

"Email it to me and I'll send it to the captain," Dane said. "If we're lucky, maybe one of the other firefighters saw him hanging around the hotel or apartment building."

Skye sent it to Dane's phone, then stared at the picture of the two men who had played such a big role in her life the past few years. It was hard to believe that one of them might be dead and the other was trying to kill her.

* * * * *

Dinner with Dane was interesting. At least that was the best word Jax could come up with to describe it. Tense, uncomfortable, and painful were words that also fit.

As they ate the amazing meal Skye had made—proof she could cook as well as bake—it was obvious Dane had to work hard to hold his tongue. Jax had to admit he was impressed. His friend wasn't usually very good at keeping his mouth shut.

While Dane didn't come right out and say it, he clearly still didn't like Jax dating his little sister. Skye tried to ignore the scowls her brother sent in their direction whenever they touched or kissed, but even she couldn't pretend when Dane asked for a pillow and blanket so he could sleep on the couch.

"Why don't you just sleep in the guest bedroom?" Skye asked, glancing over her shoulder at him as she closed the dishwasher and turned it on.

"If I sleep there, where are you going to sleep?" Dane demanded.

She gave him a look that said, *Duh*. "In Jax's bed, you dope. Where'd you think?" Before Dane could reply, she went up on her toes to kiss Jax on the lips. "You coming?"

Jax nodded. "I'll be there in a minute."

Skye hesitated, as if she was worried he and Dane might get into another fight. After a moment, she gave him a smile and told her brother to have a good night, then walked down the hallway and into the bedroom, Rodeo at her heels.

"This thing between you and my sister—you really care for her, don't you?" Dane asked.

Jax nodded. "Yeah, I do. Is that going to be a problem?"

Dane considered the question for a moment. "I don't know yet."

With that, he turned and strode down the hallway, disappearing into the guest room and quietly closing the door.

Jax swore under his breath, then went to make sure the doors were locked. Okay, so maybe he had violated the guy code when he decided to sleep with his best friend's sister, but pissing off Dane was a small price to pay for being with Skye. He'd been with his share of women both on the rodeo circuit and after joining the fire department—for some reason, the opposite sex seemed to have a thing for cowboys and firefighters—but none of them could hold a candle to Skye. She was the first woman he could picture spending the rest of his life with, and if Dane didn't like it, that was too damn bad.

Turning off the lights, Jax headed for the bedroom. Skye was already in bed, Rodeo stretched out along the bottom with his head on his paws.

"Since I didn't hear any furniture breaking, I guess it's safe to assume you and Dane didn't get into another fight," she said.

Jax felt a smile tug at the corner of his mouth as he yanked his T-shirt over his head. "He might not be ready to give us his blessing yet, but he's coming around."

Skye didn't say anything, but instead watched silently while he finished undressing.

He ducked into the bathroom to brush his teeth, then slipped into bed beside her. She scooted eagerly into his arms, curling up beside him and resting her cheek against his chest.

"Promise me you'll be careful," she said softly. "If Jordan was the one who attacked you this morning, he might try again. I don't know what I'd do if something happened to you, Jax."

He tightened his arm around her and pressed a kiss to her silky hair. "Nothing is going to happen to me, Skye. I promise."

Nothing was going to happen to her, either. If Jordan got within ten feet of Skye, that asshole was going to have to deal with him, and Jax would do anything to protect her.

Chapter Eight

JAX PULLED HIS motorcycle into Station 58's lot and parked, then shoved down the kickstand and killed the engine. Captain Stewart had called an hour ago and told him the arson investigators and cops wanted to talk to him about the guy who had assaulted him and whether it could be Skye's ex-boyfriend. Jax wasn't thrilled about being separated from Skye, but at least Dane was there to keep an eye on her. Skye had wanted to come with him, saying she might be able to help the investigation, but there was no way in hell he was letting her leave the ranch any more than necessary while Jordan was out there. The nut job had resorted to using fire in his first two attacks, but there was nothing to say the guy wouldn't use a gun next time.

Jax found the captain in the training room with a few people from the fire investigation division, some uniformed police officers, and a detective.

After introductions were made, the detective—Collins—put the photo of Jordan that Skye had given them up on the training room's projector screen. Then he went through everything the NYPD had sent down.

"I'm going to bottom line this," Collins said. "The NYPD still can't find Jordan McAvoy or Aiden Dunn. Based on evidence at McAvoy's apartment, they think he killed Dunn and got rid of the body. They assume McAvoy then left New York to come to Dallas to get back at Skye Chandler for leaving him by setting fire to the hotel where she was staying. Unfortunately, they have no evidence McAvoy ever boarded a plane in New York or at any of the other nearby airports, either. They also can't find evidence of him leaving on a train or bus or rental car."

Jax swore silently. "Why the hell do we care how he got out of New York? We know he's here. We need to find him before he finds Skye."

"That's the problem—we don't *know*. We *think* he's here. Just like we think he's after Skye, and now you." Collins shook his head. "But no one has seen McAvoy for sure and we have nothing to convince anyone that the arson cases are even linked to each other, much less to Skye and you."

Stewart frowned. "So what the hell are you saying?"

"I'm saying that the police department can't dedicate much in the way of manpower to this case or assign any kind of protective detail to Skye Chandler."

Jax snorted. "You'd rather wait until she ends up dead, I guess."

Collins let out an expletive. "That's not what we want and you know it." He sighed. "I'll have patrol do extra drive-bys of your ranch. For now, that's all we can do."

Jax would have argued, but just then Tory walked in to tell the captain that the chief was on the phone looking for an update on the situation.

As Stewart left the room, Tory walked over to study the picture of Skye, Jordan, and Aiden that was still up on the screen. "So this is the guy who started those fires and tried to kill you and Dane's sister, huh? And he looks so normal."

Jax scowled at the picture of Jordan. "I don't know. Underneath that blond hair and spray-on tan, he looks like some kind of serial killer to me."

Tory frowned. "Blond hair? Which guy are you looking at?"

Jax pointed to Jordan. "Him. He's the psycho ex-boyfriend trying to kill Skye."

"If he's the ex-boyfriend, who the hell is that?" Tory asked, motioning to Aiden.

"That's Skye's best friend, Aiden."

Tory looked at Jax like he was crazy. "Huh. Well, if that guy is the psycho ex-

126

boyfriend, what was the other one doing in the hotel the night of the fire?"

Jax hadn't realized anyone else had been listening to their conversation until the entire room suddenly went quiet.

"Aiden was there?" he asked. "Are you sure?"

"Yeah." Tory looked at the photo again. "I found him up on the fifth floor a little while after you came down with Skye. He'd collapsed from smoke inhalation."

Collins shared a look with his fellow DPD officers before moving closer to the screen and jabbing a finger at Aiden. "You're positive this is the man?"

Tory nodded. "Yeah. I mean, it's not as dramatic as getting to save a beautiful woman, but I did lug the guy down five flights of stairs and across a parking lot. It kind of makes a man's face easy to remember."

Collins muttered something under his breath. "No wonder the NYPD couldn't find any evidence of McAvoy leaving New York—he never did."

"Shit," Jax muttered. "That means Aiden is probably the one trying to kill Skye."

The detective pulled out his cell phone. "I'm going to call this in. Get a BOLO out on Dunn."

"I thought you said Aiden was Skye's friend?" Tory said to Jax. "Why would he try to kill her?"

Jax pulled out his own phone and slid his thumb across the screen to unlock it. "Who the fuck cares? I need to call Dane and let him know what's going on."

But when he called Dane's cell, it immediately went to voice mail. Jax swore and called him again, but it did the same thing. "Dane, it's me. Aiden is the guy after Skye, not Jordan."

He texted the same message for good measure before calling his home landline. He swore when he got the answering machine.

"Shit!" he hissed. "Dane's not picking up his cell and I got the answering machine when I called my home phone. That can't be a coincidence. I need to get over there."

As he raced out of the room, Jax heard the detective telling the uniformed cops to go with him even as Collins called in for the closest patrol unit to get to the ranch. Jax didn't even slow down. He might not be a cop, but that wasn't going to stop him from protecting Skye and Dane.

* * * * *

Skye was in the kitchen, trying out the new cupcake recipe she'd picked up last night on the internet—chocolate with a bacon and marshmallow cream filling—when Dane came in. He'd avoided her since Jax left, so she fully expected him to walk right past her and grab something from the fridge, then walk straight back out without saying a word. But after getting a soda, he walked over to the island where she was working.

"Mind if I try one?" he asked, motioning to the last batch of cupcakes she'd just taken out of the oven.

"Sure, go ahead. Careful though, they're still a little hot."

He nodded and unpeeled the wrapper, taking an insanely large bite and chewing it as if the filling was room temperature. Then he raised an eyebrow. "Hey, this is actually pretty good."

She knew she shouldn't let it, but for whatever reason, his surprised tone pissed her off so bad she almost threw a marshmallow covered spoon at him.

"You don't have to act so shocked," she said. "I realize you think I'm an idiot for quitting my job to bake cupcakes, but I do know what I'm doing."

Her brother looked like he was about to argue, then had the decency to look contrite. "I didn't mean it that way."

She tossed the mixing spoon back in the bowl so hard that some of the filling slopped over the side. She ignored it. "Then how did you mean it, Dane? Because I'd really like to know."

She expected him to get defensive. It was what he'd done any time she called him out about anything since they were kids. But he didn't. Instead, he gazed at her with a sadness in his eyes she'd never seen before, not even when their parents had died.

"I just meant that I'm sorry," he finally said. "I know I haven't been the kind of brother you needed since Mom and Dad died, but I really tried."

Skye stared at him, dumbfounded for a moment. Then she ran around the cupcake covered island and threw her arms around her brother, squeezing him tightly.

"What the hell are you talking about?" she demanded. "You're the best brother a girl could ever have."

Dane laughed as he hugged her back. "Yeah, right."

"You are," she insisted.

He pulled away to look at her. "I know I said some really shitty stuff when you came back to Dallas. I'm sorry about that, too. But I'm even sorrier about shipping you away to college right after Mom and Dad died without ever asking if it was what you wanted."

She felt tears burn her eyes, and quickly blinked them back. The day Dane had put her on a plane for college had almost been as bad as the day they'd lost their parents. Hearing he'd been hurting just as much made her feel like a bitch for thinking all the terrible things she had about him.

"Let's just forget about that, okay? It's in the past." She gave him a small smile. "Besides, I understand why you did it. You thought it would be best to get me away from home and all the bad memories. I get it."

Dane shook his head. "I wish I could look you in the eye and tell you that's why I sent you off to college, but I'd be lying to you, and to myself."

"What do you mean?"

He picked up another cupcake, but instead of eating it, he stared at it pensively. He was silent for so long, she didn't think he was ever going to answer. But finally, he took a deep breath and looked at her.

"I didn't ship you off to college for your benefit, Skye. I did it for mine. Because every time I looked at you and saw how unhappy you were, it was a reminder that Mom and Dad were dead because of me."

Skye reeled back as if her brother had slapped her. Dane was home when the fire had started, but that didn't mean he was responsible—even indirectly. She refused to believe that.

"Don't say that," she pleaded. "The fire was an accident. It was nobody's fault they died. It was just a stupid, horrible accident."

"The fire was an accident. Faulty wiring." Dane's mouth tightened. "But what happened afterward was all on me."

Her brother looked so torn and broken right then that her heart broke for him. It was obvious he'd been carrying this pain around for a long time. She only wished she understood why.

"Dane, what are you saying?"

He turned his attention back to the cupcake again and carefully peeled off the wrapper. Like he didn't want to waste any of the cake by letting it get stuck to the paper.

"I was in the basement playing video games when I smelled the smoke," he said softly, not looking at her. "I thought Mom had burned something in the oven, so I didn't pay any attention. Then I heard the flames. When I ran upstairs, the whole first floor was on fire. I still don't know why the smoke alarms never went off—nobody ever figured out that part. I shouted for Mom and Dad, yelling for them to get outside."

He stopped to wipe tears from his eyes with the heel of his hand. "I was sure they heard me, so I ran outside. I didn't see them right away, so I ran around the whole house. That was when I realized they hadn't come out, that they were still in there. I ran back inside and tried to get up the steps, but it was too late. The fire had run up the walls and collapsed the whole landing, crushing the stairs."

The tears he couldn't seem to shed ran freely down Skye's face. She put her arm around her brother's broad shoulders. "None of that was your fault, Dane. You did all you could. No one could have made it up those stairs, even in full firefighter's gear."

He shook his head. "I could have gotten up those stairs and gotten to them in time if I hadn't panicked and run out of the house first."

"You were barely out of high school, Dane. You did what any eighteen-year-old would have done. You shouted for Mom and Dad to get out of the house, then you got out yourself. I never held you accountable for their deaths. Nobody did."

"Maybe not, but I held myself accountable," he said. "After becoming a firefighter and talking to some people, I realized how stupid that was. But back then, every time I saw you staring off in the distance with tears in your eyes, or heard you crying in your bed at night, all I could think was that it was my fault. So, when people told me that Mom and Dad would have wanted you to go to college, I figured that it would probably be best for both of us if you left Dallas, but especially me. That way I wouldn't have to look at you and remember what I did."

Skye wiped the tears from her cheeks with her fingers. "Why didn't you ever tell me any of this?"

He looked at her, his eyes still wet. "Probably the same reason you never mentioned you'd rather make cupcakes than work on Wall Street—because we were both so caught up in our own issues that we didn't bother seeing things from the other's perspective."

She gave him a wry smile. "We're some screwed up siblings, aren't we?"

He laughed and gave her a hug. "Yeah. But I think we're getting better. And your cupcakes really are good. Mom would be proud."

Skye liked to think so.

Dane leaned back against the island, watching as she frosted the rest of the cupcakes. For the first time in almost forever, they simply talked—about college, why she'd left her job on Wall Street, and how the events with their parents' death had made Dane want to become a firefighter. It was an amazing few hours. Skye felt like she was meeting her brother for the very first time.

After his fourth cupcake, Dane announced he was going to check outside to make sure everything was quiet. Skye thought that was an unnecessary risk, but knew she'd never talk her brother out of it. They might be in a good place after their heartfelt conversation, but Dane still wasn't going to take that kind of advice from his little sister.

"Be careful," she warned. "And take your phone."

"I will." He grabbed his cell from the counter. "Keep the door locked."

Skye finished cleaning the mixing bowl and set it in the dish rack to dry, then opened Jax's laptop so she could do some detailed break-even analyses of her newest cupcake. While it tasted great, she needed to figure out how much it would cost to make based on the ingredients, as well as how much money she could expect to make by selling them. It wasn't nearly as much fun as baking, but it was just as important to her new business as how good a cupcake tasted.

She was so wrapped up in the numbers she didn't hear her brother come back until he knocked on the door. Beside her, Rodeo was immediately on his feet, his ears lifted and his eyes trained on the door.

"It's okay, boy," she told him as she slid off the stool. "Dane just forgot to take the key with him."

Rodeo must have wanted to see for himself because he walked to the door with her. She undid the lock and opened it, a smart-aleck remark on her lips, only to jump when she saw that it wasn't Dane.

"Aiden! Oh my God, I thought you were dead!"

Opening the door wide, she threw herself into his arms. Tears filled her eyes. She was so relieved to see him alive and okay. Blinking, she took a step back, then grabbed his hand and tugged him inside as she closed the door. Beside her, Rodeo growled.

"Rodeo, this is Aiden," she said, reaching down to pat the dog on his head. "He's a friend."

Rodeo growled again, this time baring his teeth. Aiden tensed.

She gave Aiden an embarrassed look. "Sorry. He's never like this. I'll go put him in the bedroom."

Skye hooked her fingers in Rodeo's collar and gently but firmly led him away from Aiden. Rodeo resisted, barking the whole way to the bedroom and refusing to take his eyes off Aiden. When she finally got him inside, she ordered him to sit and told him to behave, then closed the door.

Aiden was standing where she'd left him, still looking a little nervous.

"Sorry about that. Rodeo is usually so good with people." She studied his face. He looked pale and his eyes had dark circles under them, like he hadn't slept in days. "Aiden, what happened between you and Jordan? The cops in New York told me that you were missing. Someone called them to say you and Jordan had gotten into a fight at his apartment. The police thought he killed you."

"He tried." Aiden ran his hand through his curly, dark hair. "Jordan's out of his mind, Skye. After you left, he went crazy, saying he was going to come down here and kill you. That if he couldn't have you, no one could."

She shuddered. Jax and Dane had been right. From what Aiden said, it sounded like Jordan was more far gone than any of them had thought. She was just grateful Aiden hadn't been hurt.

"I need to call the police and tell them that Jordan is definitely in Dallas."

She turned to go into the kitchen, but Aiden caught her arm.

"We don't have time. Jordan's already on his way here."

"How...?"

Aiden shook his head. "I don't know how he found you. He must have followed your new boyfriend from the fire station. Maybe even your brother. Who knows? Right now, it doesn't matter. We need to get you out of here before he shows up."

He tightened his hold on her hand and pulled her toward the door.

"Aiden, wait! I can't just leave. My brother's here."

Aiden glanced over his shoulder at her, but didn't stop. "Your brother's fine. I talked to him when I first got here. He's waiting for us outside."

Skye let him lead her out the door and down the steps to a dark blue minivan. If her head wasn't spinning, she would have laughed at the idea of Aiden driving a minivan, even if it was a rental.

They were halfway there when she realized Dane was nowhere in sight. She slowed her steps. What if Jordan was already here? What if he'd hurt her brother?

She looked around, her eyes lingering on her brother's truck before turning to Aiden. "Where's Dane?"

Aiden practically dragged her the rest of the way to the minivan. "He must have gone in the barn to get something. I'll find him. Let's get you in the van first. I don't like you out in the open like this."

He hit a button on his key fob and opened the sliding door on the passenger side, then shoved her in the second row of seats and leaned in to buckle her seatbelt for her. What the hell? She wasn't a five-year-old.

"I need to borrow your phone," she said. "I have to let my boyfriend know what's going on."

Aiden's clicked her seat belt into place, his hands stilling on the metal as he lifted his head to look at her. "You mean Jax? We can call him as soon as I get you someplace safe."

Skye was about to say okay when something struck her. "How do you know Jax's name?"

Aiden stared at her for a moment, then looked away. "You mentioned him to me a few times back in New York."

Ducking out of the minivan, he slammed the door closed, then ran around the front of the vehicle. Instead of going into the barn to look for her brother, though, he opened the driver's door and got in. Suddenly, everything that had felt so right a mere sixty seconds ago now felt completely wrong.

She'd never told Aiden or anyone else in New York about Jax. Not even her girlfriends. While she'd always harbored a serious crush on him, his name had absolutely never come up in conversation once. Why would it? It's not like Aiden would have been interested in hearing about a hunky cowboy from Dallas with six-pack abs and irresistible dimples.

A wave of suspicion crawled up her back. She slowly reached down, unbuckling her seat belt as quietly as she could. "Aren't you going to get my brother, Aiden?"

He glanced at her in the rearview mirror as he put the keys in the ignition. "He can meet up with us later. I need to get you out of here."

The suspicion gripping her was edged with fear now. She locked eyes with Aiden in the mirror. "How did you know I was at the ranch?"

He tore his gaze away from hers, but not before she saw his dark eyes harden. "Jordan told me before he left New York. He called your brother. Dane said you were staying with some guy you knew back in high school. I think that's what really set Jordan off and made him come after you, knowing you were sleeping with another man."

Her heart dropped into her stomach. Dane said Jordan had called the day after the fire at the hotel. If her ex-boyfriend had started the fire, he would already have been in Dallas, which meant Aiden was lying his ass off.

It also meant Aiden was the one who'd tried to kill her and Jax. No wonder Rodeo didn't like him.

Aiden must have realized she was onto him because he reached for the lock button at the same moment she grabbed the handle of the sliding door. If she hadn't already unbuckled her seat belt, she wouldn't have had a snowball's chance in hell of making it.

Skye hit the ground outside the van and was running for the barn before Aiden even got out.

"Skye, stop!" he shouted. "Don't go in there!"

She ignored him and kept running until she got to the barn where Jax kept the farm equipment. She looked around wildly for her brother, but all she saw was a gigantic tractor, lawn mowers, and every kind of power tool imaginable. The place smelled to high heaven with gasoline and grease, and she had to fight back a cough.

"Dane, are you in here?" she shouted.

When he didn't answer, she called his name again. Still nothing.

She ran toward the back of the barn, becoming more convinced with every step that her brother had never come in here, when she rounded the side of the big John Deere tractor and tripped over Dane's body.

Skye screamed as she hit the floor, not in pain but out of terror that her brother was dead. She pushed herself up from the dirt and scrambled over to Dane. She knew from the first-aid class she'd taken in college that she shouldn't move him because she could hurt him even more, but she gently rolled him over onto his back anyway. She had to know if he was alive. Tears spilled onto her cheeks when she saw the blood flowing from a gash along the left side of his head. But then she saw his chest slowly rise and fall, and she sagged with relief.

She pressed her hand to the wound, hoping to stop the blood, when Aiden came around the tractor. She lifted her head to glare at him.

"Why did you do this?" she demanded. "I thought you were my friend, damn you!"

"I was your fucking friend," he ground out. "But I wanted to be more than that!"

Skye was still reeling from that when Aiden took a coil of rope from a hook on the wall and advanced on her. She tried to defend herself with one hand while keeping the other pressed to the wound on Dane's head, but Aiden grabbed her arm and dragged her away from her brother.

She fought like crazy, trying to punch him with both fists, but as mad as she was, she wasn't nearly strong enough to do any damage. Aiden caught her flailing arms and tied her hands in front of her, then shoved her back against the wall of the barn so hard she fell. She hit the ground hard, the breath exploding from her lungs.

She lay there gasping for air, trying to twist her wrists free as Aiden yanked her arms above her head and tied the end of the rope to a hook on the wall. Then he stood there glaring down at her.

"Do you really think I spent all that time convincing you to dump that jackass Jordan just so you could come back here and jump into bed with that walking cliché you're sleeping with?"

He took a step toward her and she couldn't help but flinch. He immediately stopped and held up his hands in what he probably thought was a placating gesture. But it was hard to think of him as calm and reasonable when he'd just tied her up and hit her brother on the head.

"When you told me you wanted to quit working in investments and start a bakery, I thought you'd do it in New York," he said. "I was ready to help you, figuring we would do it together. I'd been waiting for years for you to see that Jordan was just using you, and when you finally did, you just up and left."

She was tempted to point out that he had encouraged her to chase her dreams, then decided that wasn't a very good idea. "You killed Jordan, didn't you?"

The sudden change of subject seemed to catch Aiden off guard for a moment. But then he shrugged. "He didn't really leave me much choice. I stopped by to talk to him and the bastard said he was getting ready to fly down to Dallas to beg you to take him back. I had to kill him to protect you from falling for his crap and getting sucked back into his life. I stuffed him in the trash chute in his apartment building. They'll be lucky if they ever find the body."

The really scary part—beyond the fact that he'd killed the man who was supposed to be his best friend—was that Aiden clearly believed what he was saying. That he thought he'd somehow saved her by murdering Jordan.

"And the fire in the hotel?" she asked softly. "Was that to protect me, too?"

At least he had the sanity left to look a little chagrined at that. "I didn't mean for that to happen. I just wanted to start a little fire so I could rescue you and show you what kind of man I could be for you. But the fire got out of control. I still tried to save you, but that oversized pile of muscles got there before me."

There were just so many things wrong with that entire line of thinking that it was impossible to point out all of them. Not that she would have anyway. She didn't want to piss him off anymore.

"How did you find me at that hotel anyway?" she asked.

If she could keep Aiden talking, there was a chance Dane would wake up. She hoped.

"I put a GPS tracking app on your phone." His mouth edged up in a wry smile. "I'm in IT, remember?"

She wasn't sure what she'd expected him to say, but it sure as hell wasn't that. But before she could tell him what a complete dirtbag he was, he walked behind her to the far end of the barn and started doing something that made a lot of noise. She craned her neck to see what he was doing, but it was no use.

"Unfortunately, your phone got destroyed in the hotel fire," he said conversationally. "So I was forced to call your dim-witted brother and pretend I was Jordan to get him to tell me where you were staying.

I have to admit, I was fucking pissed off when I realized you'd hooked up with some muscle-bound cowboy who likes to play with fire. I thought you were better than that. Guess I had you all wrong."

Aiden came back into her line of vision, a tin gas can in his hand. It sloshed loudly as he walked toward her. Skye's heart began to pound. What the hell was he going to do with that?

He dropped to one knee on the ground and pulled off the top of the small spout, then tore a piece of cloth from the dirty white rag in his hand and stuffed it into the opening. Even from where she sat against the wall a few feet away, Skye could smell the gas fumes coming from the can.

He glanced at her as he tossed the rest of the rag on the floor. "What? You didn't think I was just going to let you go, did you? I mean, I tried to get you to come with me, but you wanted to stay with your brother."

He glanced at Dane, still passed out cold on the ground. That's when Skye realized Aiden had never been the friend she'd thought he was. He had played her just as much, if not more, than Jordan ever had.

"You have to admit there's a certain irony to burning you to death," he added. "Since you're sleeping with a fireman and all."

"You're not going to get away with this." She sounded like a B-grade movie, but she didn't care. She couldn't let Aiden set fire to the barn. "They'll figure out it was you."

"I doubt that." Aiden stood up and took a lighter from his pocket. "Like you said, everyone thinks Jordan killed me. I'll just show up in New York in a few days with a nasty head wound and say I don't remember anything. I'll make sure I cry at your funeral, though."

He was just about to flick the wheel on the lighter when the sounds of approaching sirens filtered through the barn.

Skye's heart leaped. She opened her mouth and screamed as loudly as she could, praying someone would hear her.

Cursing, Aiden shoved the lighter back in his pocket. He reached down and picked up a length of rag he'd tossed on the floor earlier, then walked over to her.

She kicked out with her legs, but Aiden simply brushed them aside and reached out to slam her head back against the wall. It hurt like hell and knocked her so dizzy that she couldn't do anything but sit there helplessly as he stuffed the rag in her mouth and wrapped the ends around her head to tie it in place.

"I'm sorry it had to end this way," he said as he walked back to the gas can and lit the scrap of fabric hanging out of it. "If you'd just stayed in New York with me, everything would have been different."

Skye watched through blurred vision as he tossed the can toward the far corner of the barn. There was a thud and a whoosh, then the roar of fire reached her ears. In the back of her mind, she remembered Dane telling her that flames made noise, and willed him to hear them now. But her brother didn't move. She pulled at the ropes, but that only tightened them around her wrists even more. Hot tears burned her eyes as she realized how useless it was to struggle. She and Dane were going to die just like their parents had. And all she could do was sit there while Aiden turned and walked out, leaving them to burn.

Chapter Nine

THE TWO POLICE cruisers jerked in front of Jax the moment he stopped in front of his house. He was off his bike in a flash, but the cops were right behind him, telling him to stay outside as they ran up the front porch and kicked in the door. The urge to follow behind them was overwhelming, but he held back, knowing all he would do was get in the way.

Besides, if he'd gone into the house, he wouldn't have seen the smoke coming from the equipment barn.

Shit. There were enough fuel and petroleum products to blow the whole barn off its foundation.

Jordan—Aiden—whoever—had used fire to try to kill Skye once before. It couldn't be a coincidence that one of his barns was burning now.

Jax raced toward the building, ignoring the flames rushing up the far wall as he ran inside. Another few minutes and the place would be burnt to the ground. The thought of Skye dying in there made his gut clench. She was alive. She had to be.

"Skye!"

He couldn't hear much over the roar of the fire, which was consuming the back of the barn at a rapid pace already. But he wasn't leaving until he checked everywhere. He ran around the tractor, almost stumbling when he caught sight of Skye bound and gagged and tied to a hook on the wall. Her eyes were wet with tears and she looked terrified as hell, but she was okay.

Thank God.

He slid to his knees in front of her, yanking the nasty rag up and over her head. He started to untie her wrists, but she shook her head, her eyes going wide.

Jax turned just in time see the barn doors slam shut.

Fuck.

He ran over to the doors and shoved, but they wouldn't budge.

What the hell?

He peeked through the cracks of the doors to figure out what was blocking them and saw a dark blue minivan parked up against them. He and Skye were trapped.

Ignoring the smoke threatening to choke him, Jax sprinted over to Skye, kneeling down to untie the rope from her wrists. She'd yanked so hard trying to get free that the rough hemp had chaffed them bloody.

"Dane is hurt," she shouted over the roar of the flames. "By the tractor."

Jax glanced over and saw Dane lying on the ground, dried blood covering the side of his head. Oh, damn.

Grabbing Skye's hand, he tugged her to her feet. Coughing, she kneeled beside Dane while Jax checked for a pulse. It was still beating steadily, but a pulse wouldn't help much if they didn't get out of here soon. If the flames got to the barn's fuel tanks, they were all dead.

Jax spun around, looking for a way out as his eyes watered from the smoke. Why the hell had he only put one door in this place when he built it? Because he'd been worried about someone coming in stealing the equipment, especially the tractor.

Shit, that was it!

He slid his arms underneath Dane's. "Help me get him on the tractor," he shouted at Skye.

She gave him a confused look, but hurriedly did as he asked. "How are we going to get out with the door blocked?"

"We make a new door."

The John Deere wasn't exactly made for passengers, but he'd never taken the big rotary mowing attachment off the back from when he'd mowed last, and it had plenty of space for Skye and Dane.

Skye waited for him to get Dane positioned, then climbed on beside her brother.

"Hold onto him," Jax said. "This might get rough."

The barn was so full of smoke by now he could barely see the key to start the tractor. But the moment he turned it, the engine rumbled to life. He shoved the tractor into gear and popped the clutch, aiming the John Deere toward the door, just to the left of where the minivan was parked.

The heavy front end of the tractor slammed into the left vertical support beam of the door. It might move slowly, but the tractor was damn heavy, not to mention powerful. It smashed through the support beam and the heavy boards attached to it, hitting the corner of the minivan and pushing it aside as he kept going. A few pieces of burning wood showered down on him, but luckily nothing hit him, or Skye and Dane. He kept the big wheels churning, picking up speed and moving away from the fire engulfed barn, not stopping until he got far enough away for them to be safe.

He turned to check on Skye and Dane when a flash of movement in the middle of the horse pasture caught his attention. It was Aiden. And he was running for the main road. Apparently, he'd figured out his scheme to kill them had failed. He was probably rethinking the wisdom of using his only means of transportation to block the doors of the barn because he wasn't a very fast runner.

Jax considered going after him with the tractor, then changed his mind. Not only would that mean driving through the pasture fence, but it would also mean bouncing Skye and Dane around on the mower like a couple beans in a coffee can.

"Where are you going?" Skye yelled as he jumped off the tractor and over the rail fencing around the pasture.

Jax pretended he didn't hear her. Skye would be pissed at him for chasing after a psychopath like this, but there was no way in hell he was going to let that asshole get away.

Putting two fingers in his mouth, Jax cut loose with the same loud whistle he used when he put oats out in the evening. Six horses lifted their heads, then came running. He wrapped his fingers in the mane of the first horse that got there—a big stallion named Thor—then he jumped up and threw his leg over the horse's back. Thor bucked a few times, clearly not thrilled with the idea of being ridden bareback. But after a moment, he finally settled down and took off in the direction Jax urged him.

Thor was big, and he was fast. Aiden didn't stand a chance in the big, open field. Jax caught up and ran him down in twenty seconds. At least Thor didn't stomp on the asshole as he ran him over.

Jax let the big horse keep going for another hundred feet or so, then got him slowed down and turned around. He walked the horse back to where Aiden was lying on the ground, twisting and rolling in pain. Jax slipped down from Thor's back and patted him on the rump to send him back to join the rest of the herd where they stood watching the whole scene play out with interest. By the time Thor rejoined them, they'd gone back to grazing.

Jax was hoping Aiden would give him some trouble because he really wanted to punch the hell out of the guy for all the shit he'd put Skye through. But one of Thor's hooves had clipped the back of Aiden's head and the man didn't have a clue what the hell was going on, much less his own name at the moment. Dreading the walk back, but knowing he had to do it, Jax bent down and picked Aiden up, then threw him over his shoulder and headed for the fence.

Skye, Dane, and the cops were all waiting there for him. Jax was happy to see his best friend standing, though he didn't look too steady.

The police officers took Aiden off his hands, cuffing him and leading him to their cruiser. As soon as they were gone, Skye threw herself into Jax's arms.

"Don't you ever do anything that crazy again!" she said.

Dane snorted. "What crazy part are you talking about exactly? Driving a tractor through the door of a burning barn with his girl and best friend riding on the mower attachment? Or riding a horse bareback to chase down a murderer?"

"Both," Skye said.

Going up on tiptoe, she planted a big kiss on Jax. He knew he shouldn't do it with her brother right there, but Jax said the hell with Dane and wrapped his arms around her, kissing her back. God, he loved her so much. And as soon as they were alone, he was going to damn well tell her.

"I guess I'm going to have to get used to this, huh?" Dane asked drily.

Skye pulled back, but didn't leave the circle of Jax's arms as she gave her brother a smile. "Yes, you most definitely are."

* * * * *

Jax sat back against the fence, his arm around Skye and her head on his shoulder as they watched the equipment barn burn. The fire department had arrived, but the building was a goner and so was all the equipment in it.

"Can you afford to replace both the barn and all the equipment?" Dane asked from the other side of Skye.

A paramedic had looked at Dane's head and was adamant he was going to need some stitches and maybe even a night in the hospital to run a concussion protocol. Dane had promised he'd go as soon as the fire was out. Jax intended to make sure he did.

"Yeah," he said in answer to his friend's question. "Thankfully, I carry full insurance on the place. There were a couple things I was thinking about changing anyway."

Skye lifted her head from his shoulder to regard him thoughtfully. "How much change did you have in mind?"

Chapter Ten

SKYE LAY STRETCHED out on top of Jax, his hard cock still buried deep inside her as she tried to catch her breath from another one of those amazing orgasms he seemed able to bring out of her at will. Her cheek rested on his muscled chest, making it easy for her ear to pick up the rapid-fire heartbeat that confirmed he'd come just as hard as she had. She was never going to get tired of having sex with him.

"I love you," she whispered.

He ran his fingers down her back, making her shiver. "I love you, too."

She sighed, wishing they could stay in bed all day. But then she glanced at the clock on the bedside table. Her eyes went wide. "Dang it, Jax! You kept me in bed late again. I was supposed to be packing the truck for today's deliveries already."

She quickly pushed herself up into a sitting position, which only served to drive his

155

cock deeper into her pussy, ripping long groans from both of them. As she tried to build up the energy to slide off him, his strong hands settled on her hips.

"Oh, no you don't," she said, smacking his hands away and carefully climbing off him. It was tough to do, but she knew from experience that if she let him get his hands on her and he started guiding her up and down on him, they wouldn't be getting out of this bed for another hour.

Jax chuckled, but let her go. She hopped out of the bed and ran for the en suite bathroom, sidestepping Rodeo where he lazed on the floor.

"It's not my fault I can't get enough of you. I admit it. I'm obsessed with my fiancée," he said.

Skye couldn't help but smile as she ran her brush through her hair. She and Jax had been engaged for a month now and he took great care in reminding her of that fact frequently.

He'd proposed to her two months to the day after she officially moved in with him, which had been the day after Aiden tried to kill them. Of course, she'd said yes. That meant she now had to add planning a wedding to her already crazy busy to-do list. Not that she was complaining. She was so in love with Jax that the idea of being married to him still made her giddy with excitement every time she thought about it. After what they'd gone through to be together, planning a wedding while getting her new business up and running would be a snap.

She brushed her teeth as fast as she could, then quickly put on her make-up. When she came out of the bathroom, Jax was pulling on his uniform. She would never be comfortable knowing his job involved running into burning buildings, but she trusted his abilities and knew the people he worked with—including her brother—watched out for each other like family.

Still, as they headed for the door after breakfast, she said the same thing to him she said every morning. "You're going to be careful on this shift, right?"

He pulled her into his arms just like he did every morning. "I promise to be careful. I have the most beautiful woman in the world I love more than anything waiting for me at home."

She kissed him, then together they walked outside. He headed for his pickup truck while she walked across the newly paved-in parking area toward her shop and the Comfort Cakes delivery van parked in front of it.

The equipment barn that had burned to the ground had been replaced with a new bakery barn, and while the back part still had some storage for tools, the entire front side was a full-service kitchen. Jax had taken the money from the insurance pay-off, added in a good chuck of his own cash and invested in her new company. She'd been a little worried about letting him put his personal money into the business, but he'd been adamant. She had to admit, having her shop fifty feet from the house was a heck of a lot more convenient than using some rented space on the far side of Dallas.

She unlocked the door to her shop and was immediately hit with the mouth-watering aroma of freshly baked goodies. The shop had only been up and running for about six weeks, but Jax, Dane, and the other firefighters at Station 58 had gotten the word out about her new business, and she was already starting to have a hard time keeping up with all the orders coming in. The wedding and catering jobs were the backbone of her current workload—just like her business model had suggested—but she'd also recently signed contracts to provide cupcakes, bagels, and other baked goods to several conference centers in town. Their steady demand was only going to grow as word spread. She'd probably need to hire a delivery person and a baking assistant just to keep up. That was a good problem to have, though.

She was just about to grab the first stack of boxes and head out to the van with them when the door of the shop opened and Jax came sweeping in.

"Did you forget something?" she asked as she picked up a big box of coconut frosted cupcakes.

He took the box out of her hands and set it on the counter. "As a matter of fact, I did."

Then he pulled her close and kissed her long and lingeringly on the lips. Skye slid her hands up the hard wall of his chest and kissed him right back. She was wondering if maybe they had time for a quickie on the counter when he pulled away with a sexy groan.

"What was that all about?" she asked breathlessly.

Jax grinned as he headed for the door. "Nothing special. Just wanted to make sure you knew how much I love you."

Skye smiled. Oh, she knew. But she wouldn't mind him showing her on a regular basis.

Want more hunky first responders?
Then check out the other books in the *Dallas Fire & Rescue Series* as well as all the books in the *Dallas Fire & Rescue Kindle World!*

SEAL of HER DREAMS, the prequel novella to the SEALs of CORONADO Series is FREE for a limited time!

All the details on how to get your copy are on Paige Tyler's website at
www.paigetylertheauthor.com

ABOUT PAIGE

Paige Tyler is a *New York Times* and *USA Today* Bestselling Author of sexy, romantic suspense and paranormal romance. She and her very own military hero (also known as her husband) live on the beautiful Florida coast with their adorable fur baby (also known as their dog). Paige graduated with a degree in education, but decided to pursue her passion and write books about hunky alpha males and the kick-butt heroines who fall in love with them.

She is represented by Bob Mecoy.

http://www.paigetylertheauthor.com

Made in the USA
San Bernardino, CA
04 April 2018